No True Justice

H. L. Wegley

Romantic Suspense

Cover Design: Samantha Fury
http://www.furycoverdesign.com/

OTHER BOOKS BY H. L. WEGLEY

Against All Enemies Series
1 Voice in the Wilderness
2 Voice of Freedom
3 Chasing Freedom

Pure Genius Series
1 Hide and Seek
2 On the Pineapple Express
3 Moon over Maalaea Bay
4 Triple Threat

Witness Protection Series
1 No Safe Place
2 No True Justice
3 Witness Protection 3 – coming soon

DEDICATION

This book is dedicated to the men and women of the FBI, and other divisions and offices of the Department of Justice, who continue to fulfill their oaths of office—those who perform their duties impartially, never placing biases or personal political preferences above their duty to act justly in service of their fellow Americans.

CONTENTS

OTHER BOOKS BY H. L. WEGLEY iii
DEDICATION iv
CONTENTS v
ACKNOWLEDGMENTS vii
Chapter 1 1
Chapter 2 11
Chapter 3 14
Chapter 4 17
Chapter 5 23
Chapter 6 25
Chapter 7 36
Chapter 8 41
Chapter 9 48
Chapter 10 51
Chapter 11 63
Chapter 12 81
Chapter 13 83
Chapter 14 92
Chapter 15 94
Chapter 16 98
Chapter 17 106
Chapter 18 114
Chapter 19 118
Chapter 20 122
Chapter 21 125
Chapter 22 130
Chapter 23 137
Chapter 24 139
Chapter 25 145
Chapter 26 151
Chapter 27 157
Chapter 28 159
Chapter 29 163
Chapter 30 170

Chapter 31 175
Chapter 32 179
Chapter 33 191
Chapter 34 203
Chapter 35 209
Chapter 36 212
Chapter 37 224
Epilogue 232
Author's Notes 242

ACKNOWLEDGMENTS

Many thanks to Linda and Jerry Fladoos for their boat tour of Lake Billy Chinook that filled my head with scenes for this story.

Thanks to Babe for listening to me read her the story at least four times and for catching the awkward words and logical errors as she listened.

Thanks to Duke Gibson for providing her thoughts on the plot and story after she voluntarily suffered through a reading of the first draft.

Thank you, Samantha Fury, for extracting all of Gemma Saint's beautiful hair from that horrible green background and placing her on the cover you designed.

And, finally, thanks to our Lord Who has, at least once more, left me with enough words and wits to fill the pages of another novel.

If we are to keep our democracy, there must be one commandment: Thou shalt not ration justice.
Judge Learned Hand

He that ruleth over men must be just, ruling in the fear of God.
2 Samuel 23:3b (KJV)

Chapter 1

July 4th, Madras, Oregon, 10:45 p.m.

Happy birthday, America! I—I still love you.

As Georgia Simpson, she did love her native land, though she could not shake the feeling that her government had done her a grave injustice.

A deep boom jarred her head and resonated in her chest.

Georgia looked upward.

The explosion filled the late evening sky with a brilliant display of red, white and blue lights that shot outward like a microcosm of the big bang. Then the lights floated downward and, within a few seconds, disappeared into the indigo sky.

And so ended the finale of the Madras Fourth of July celebration at Sahalee Park.

The crowd cheered.

The band struck up a rousing rendition of *It's a Grand Old Flag.*

Families and friends celebrated together.

But Georgia Simpson would walk home as usual ... alone. If she had to be alone tonight, she could choose not to be Georgia.

After eight months in WITSEC, she had come to loathe the name the Department of Justice had coerced her into taking.

"It's safer to keep your initials, GS," they had said.

But she was Gemma Saint. Her life as Gemma was satisfying and filled with excitement. Georgia would gladly return to being Gemma, if she had the opportunity.

The problem was, according to the DOJ, the life expectancy of Gemma Saint roughly equaled that of a free-drink award on her Starbuck's card.

As Georgia Simpson, she could continue living her lonely, mundane life in a small, Central-Oregon town, provided she avoided everything Gemma had done and loved.

Tonight, she would rebel. For the rest of the evening, she would be Gemma. After she returned to work at the hospital tomorrow, the miserable masquerade could resume.

Gemma trudged along the path that left Sahalee Park and then turned onto the dark street that led to her rented duplex three blocks away.

With no streetlights, the shadows lining the narrow avenue provided dozens of places where Castellano's creeps could be hiding, waiting for Gemma Saint.

She shivered, though the temperature was probably still in the eighties. On second thought, maybe Georgia wasn't such a bad name.

Gemma flinched when her cell buzzed her leg and then sounded the alert for an arriving message.

Who would text her at 11:00 p.m. on the Fourth of July? It was too early for that monthly text about her phone bill. And she hadn't made any friends yet. Not even at work or church. Only a few acquaintances. The curse of being introverted.

Gemma had been cursed at college too. The male students at Texas A&M had dubbed her INTJ girl. They considered the mystique of women with her rare, introverted personality type a challenge, and they had pursued Gemma *ad nauseam*.

The women students, on the other hand, considered her stuck-up and unlikeable.

Back to the present, where incoming calls or messages were rare events. She should probably check the message, though it was likely spam.

Gemma pulled her phone from her shorts pocket. The display showed the name of the most important person she knew on planet Earth, U.S. Marshal Cody Cottrell, her WITSEC Inspector. In that role, Cody wore several other hats, counselor, social worker, financial advisor—whatever Gemma needed him to be, everything except the person who could give her back the life she loved, the life of Gemma Saint.

Gemma touched the message icon, scanned the text, and sucked in a breath so hard she choked on it.

Gemma, your ID is compromised. Pack a bag now and prepare to leave. Will call in a few minutes with more instructions.

He had used her real name. Why? That was forbidden.

Only one answer explained both the message and the breach of protocol. WITSEC was over for Georgia Simpson.

But what did that mean for Gemma Saint? And why weren't marshals here escorting her to safety, to a new home and a new identity?

Other questions came. How much time did she have? She needed new ID if Georgia Simpson had been compromised. How was she supposed to get it?

The shadows around her pressed in, invading her personal space. Men like Joseph Castellano employed assassins who committed unspeakable atrocities for revenge. Was someone already here, hidden in the darkness, waiting for her?

A cat spit, screeched, and darted out of the shadows on her right.

Run Gemma!

The warning came from somewhere deep inside, more a feeling than actual words.

Gemma broke into an all-out sprint. Her runner's legs maintained that torrid pace for two and a half blocks to her rented duplex.

Breathing hard when she reached her front door, she fumbled with her key and finally unlocked the door. Once inside, she secured all three locks.

Without more information, she might make deadly mistakes. Gemma hurried to her bedroom and keyed in a reply to Marshal Cottrell's message.

How much time do I have? What about a new ID?

She pressed send.

What did she need most? Clothes.

Gemma scurried to her closet, pulled out her large duffle bag, and dumped the contents of her underwear drawer into the bag.

Her cell blasted out *Recall* from the *Texas Aggie War Hymn.* Using the fight song of her *alma mater* for her ringtone violated WITSEC rules. A small violation, but it was something that could tie Georgia to Gemma Saint. Another one of her rebellions to being forced into WITSEC.

She jumped and yelped when the drawer fell from her hands, sending a knifing pain through her foot.

Gemma limped to her bed and sat. The display on her phone said Marshal Cody Cottrell. But, if there had been compromises, she needed to be sure of the caller's identity before divulging anything.

"Hello."

"Gemma, it's Cody Cottrell. You need to—"

"Cody, what's happening?"

His sigh blasted through the phone with a static-like sound. "You've got to leave as soon as we're through talking. It's possible that my calls are being monitored."

An icy chill brought a shiver to Gemma's shoulders. "*Your* phone? Who would monitor the U.S. Marshals? And why am I in danger? Is it the mafia guy, Castellano?"

"Forget Castellano. There never was any real danger from him."

"Then why was I placed in WITSEC, Cody?" Gemma's voice crescendoed.

She had lived alone, isolated from her family, in a new world for eight long months. And Gemma had to leave her career as a journalist just as she completed her master's degree. Everything had been thrown away for nothing.

The back of her neck grew hot. Gemma would lose it, any second now, something Gemma Saint never did. She took a deep breath and blew it back out. Lashing out at Cody wouldn't help, and it wasn't his fault.

"I'm so sorry, Gemma. I'll try to explain but listen closely. We don't have much time."

No time? But she needed some time. Running for her life with no plan or destination—that was a formula for disaster.

The muddle of thoughts swirling through her mind wasn't helping. She needed to listen to Cody.

"Gemma, Marsh McDowell just won an appeal that could overturn his conviction. The Federal Prosecutor's staff and Marsh's attorneys have all gone in full attack mode for the upcoming trial."

"I worked for Marsh. I testified for him. He was innocent. Isn't that good news?"

"Not if you're an opponent of President Gramm. There are people in powerful places who do not want the president to run for a second term. After the scandals these people manufactured, Gramm isn't sure he wants to have his family drug through the sewer of another campaign. But his opponents are assuming he *will* run and—"

"And Marsh's news network is President Gramm's only hope for fair coverage. Without Marsh ..."

"Exactly. But no matter how badly they want to, no one in their right mind assassinates an American president. The people who can get him elected, on the other hand, are fair game."

"But why me? It's because of the appeal, isn't it?"

Cody sighed into the phone. "Gramm's opponents fear what may happen during the appeal. First, the watchdog organization, Guardians of Justice, recently won an FOIA lawsuit against the Department of Justice. The FBI must turn over all their records related to Marshall McDowell. If those records contain what many suspect, the records could result in charges against members of the DOJ."

It was obvious where this was headed. And that destination brought both satisfaction and danger. "Marsh's attorney will bring me out of WITSEC to testify, won't he?"

"Your testimony could swing the jury in Marsh's favor. Then Marsh goes free. He shouts the truth about this whole sordid conspiracy to the world and ..."

"And President Gramm gets re-elected." Under other circumstances, Gemma might have laughed.

It was mind-boggling to think that Gemma Saint, a twenty-four-year-old nobody, an intern at a media outlet, albeit an influential outlet, could be the person who determined the next president and, indirectly, the future of a nation that writhed in a life-and-death struggle to remain a sovereign, democratic republic. Well, she might be the deciding factor if she were alive to testify.

"It's possible our phone call is being monitored. Maybe even recorded. So we won't mention any specific times or places."

"But, Cody, don't they need a FISA Warrant to spy on American citizens? And spying on a U.S. Marshal—who would do that?"

"These people don't play by the rules, Gemma. And the corruption starts high and goes deep in the DOJ. That's all I can say, and it's all we have time for. You need to pack and leave in the next few minutes. Go anywhere where you believe no one can find you. I'm not exempt from the danger here either, so I may need to disappear too. When you get a chance, buy a burner phone and, in a few days, text your new number to the number I'll text to you in a few minutes."

"Might they intercept your text?"

"I can guarantee that they won't intercept that text."

"I'll need new ID. How do—"

"Just go to a college campus. Pretend to be a student and ask some students where you can get a fake driver's license. Someone will know. It won't be a professional job. The ID will let you make purchases, but it won't fly with law enforcement."

"But, Cody, I'm not an underage college student. I'm twenty-four."

"Yeah. But you look ..."

And she did. Gemma was slender and had a childlike face that was both a blessing and a curse. But, in this situation, it could work to her advantage.

"Thanks, Cody."

"Take care, Gemma. I'll be praying for—"

A loud report came through her phone, blasting her eardrum. Then thumping sounds.

Finally, silence.

This couldn't be happening. Maybe it was a test to see how she reacted or something the marshals were doing to improve her security.

Gemma was grasping at straws. She had heard a gunshot.

"Cody ... Cody, are you okay?"

Please answer.

A rasping noise came through the phone, then the sound of someone breathing.

"Cody, is that you?"

No reply. Only slow, deep breathing.

A guttural groan rose, involuntarily. Gemma didn't watch horror movies, but this seemed like a scene stolen from one. She pressed the icon to cut off the call.

Reality sent her mind spinning like a centrifuge, leaving only the heaviest thought. Marshal Cody Cottrell was dead, and he had died trying to save her life.

The cycle had repeated. Gemma's jinx. Whatever she did, wherever she went, she seemed to endanger people, people she cared about.

Was she broken in some way that brought evil to people? It didn't fit with her theology, but it seemed to be true.

When she was twelve, her attempt to protect her little brother, Jerry, from bullies made matters worse. Jerry ended up badly beaten and in the hospital.

A year ago, her testimony at Marsh McDowell's trial, testimony that should have cleared him, was spun by a clever federal prosecutor to convict Marsh of violating federal election campaign laws.

Now Cody.

Stop it, Gemma! You've got to think.

Cody's office was near Denver. If they killed him there, she had several hours before they could possibly reach Madras.

But when had the actual identity breach occurred? When did the wheels of this latest corrupt conspiracy start turning? She didn't know. Her safest assumption was that someone would soon arrive at her home.

Gemma sat on the edge of her bed. She was truly alone. Isolated from family. No marshal to protect her. And people in the Department of Justice wanted to kill her.

Her breathing turned to panting.

You need to calm down, Gemma Saint, and think.

Gemma took a deep breath, released it, and sought a coherent plan.

She would get new ID as Cody instructed. The campus in Bend might be the nearest place to do that.

Gemma could sell her car to one of those lots that bought any old clunker if the price was low enough. She would use the ID to purchase another car from a private party. She could leave the old plates on it and not submit the title transfer information.

Her bank account had over twenty-five thousand dollars in it, thanks to her dad. She could withdraw enough cash to buy a car from a private party.

After that, she needed a place to hide. But where would she be safe? If people in the DOJ were spying on her, no place in the United States was safe, not for very long.

Maybe *safe* wasn't a place. Maybe, for Gemma Saint, safe was a carefully planned set of circumstances, circumstances she must arrange.

Cody thought the people conspiring against the president, the ones endangering Gemma, were in the DOJ. That included the FBI. They had been involved with Marsh McDowell's trial, working with the federal prosecutor who went after Marsh on trumped-up charges. That had to be why Guardians of Justice sued for those records.

But, if it really was the FBI, or some rogue element within that organization, her only hope of ending the danger was to completely document the conspiracy and expose it in the media.

Who in the media could she trust to do that? It had to be someone known as a good investigative reporter, someone who could expose the conspiracy so thoroughly to an audience so large that the conspirators dare not come after her. Hopefully, so thoroughly that they all ended up in prison.

That was the only way she could resume life as Gemma Saint. But for now ...

I just need to be Saint Elsewhere.

She turned off her cell and dropped it in her purse.

Gemma opened another drawer and tossed the contents into her duffle bag.

One thing was certain. She needed to leave Madras, now.

Chapter 2

Max Carr opened the door to his office in the J. Edgar Hoover Building and the constant reminder that he had fallen short of his goal screamed at him from the nameplate on his desk. Deputy Director, Maximillian Carr.

The word *Deputy* needed to go. And, in about eighteen months, it would.

But another matter had erupted a few hours ago, something that could cost him his goal and possibly his career. A phone call could right the ship before it took on water. If it didn't, things could get messy ... very messy. But cleaning up a mess was preferable to going down with a sinking ship.

He pulled his secure phone from its holster and hit Agent Clarke's speed dial number. Sometime soon, before his cell was replaced or went in for repairs, he needed to delete Clarke's entry.

Max's working relationship with the analyst in the Data Intercept Technology Unit (DITU) would be questioned if found. Heaven forbid that the IG team would find it during an inspection, because Max's use of Clarke to investigate certain U.S. citizens violated several Bureau policies and, depending upon a judge's interpretation, it violated U.S. Code.

"DITU, Clarke here."

"This is Carr. I'm secure on this end. How about you?"

"I'm secure ... well, as secure as one can be in this place."

Nothing was absolutely secure around DITU. One never knew—

"Is this about the email account?"

"Yes. It seems our little saint in WITSEC has gone AWOL. Have you seen any activity?"

"Uh ... as a matter of fact, I noticed some activity a short time ago."

"Short as in a few hours?"

"No, sir. As in a few minutes."

Max was in luck. Maybe he would know where little Miss Saint was going before she got there. "Where did the message originate?"

"The message came through a router at a cheap motel in Bend, Oregon. I have the IP address."

That wasn't surprising. She had opted for a somewhat larger city to hide, at least temporarily. "Where did it go?"

"That's the strange part. She's in Bend, but the message went to a server in Bend, a server that hosts email for that Internet news site that's been stirring up trouble, The American Motto."

"Lex James!" Max muted his phone and swore, reaching for the dregs of his vocabulary, anything profane enough to express his loathing of Mr. James, the young man with a platform too big for the likes of a kid like him. Now, the little witch, Gemma Saint, was trying to save herself by exposing everything to a friendly media mogul.

"Are you there, sir? Mr. Carr?"

Max unmuted his phone. "I'm here. Just ranting a bit. Can you get me ... uh, more than the IP address?"

"More than the metadata? Sir, that would be violation of—"

"We wouldn't want to violate the Fourth Amendment. Thanks, Clarke. Please keep monitoring the metadata from the originating server—the one hosting Saint's account. And let me know, immediately, if there are more messages."

"Will do, sir."

Max ended the call and hit Agent Bladen Sikes' secure phone number.

He gave up after five rings. Maybe Blade was still in the air somewhere near Portland.

Max called again.

Blade answered on the third ring. "Sikes."

"Blade, it's Carr. The mission has changed somewhat. Saint's in the Bend area trying to contact TAM."

"That's not good, sir." Blade's deep voice rose a semitone or two.

"No, it's not. If we can't find her before she contacts TAM, Mr. Lex James might need some ... uh, special attention, too."

"Sir, if you have a long trail of bodies, it's easy to track. We need to limit the scope of this mission and leave no trail."

"Sikes, that's why I hired you. Now, do your job."

Chapter 3

Lex James pressed the post button and his editorial went live on The American Motto. "That ought to twist the Attorney General's Fruit of the Looms."

"Uncalex, whatcha' mean about twistin' the general's fruit?" The curious eyes of four-year-old Joshua gave Lex *the look*. Josh's questions wouldn't stop until that incredible curiosity, from his somewhere-north-of-two-hundred IQ was satisfied.

Caleb plopped a hand on his twin brother's shoulder. "No, Josh. It was his fruit loops."

Lex bent down, hands on knees in front of the boys. "Okay, guys. This is how it is. I posted an article to my newspaper that the head of our Justice Department won't like. That's what twisting his underwear means."

Caleb tugged on Lex's pant leg. "Uncalex, if he works for justice, he's a good man, like you. Why won't he like it?"

This could go on for an hour or more if he didn't nip it now. "Josh, Caleb, this is how it is—"

"But you already told us that." Josh's wrinkled forehead turned upward, and his wide eyes met Lex's, sucking him into those dark blue pools so deep that only the Einsteins of this world could plumb their depths.

Lex swam out of the depths, pulling hard for the surface so he wouldn't drown. "Boys ... let me explain it this way. We live in a pluralistic society where a lot of people believe different things."

"Makes'em argue, huh, Uncalex," Caleb said.

"Yeah." Josh pointed at Lex's laptop screen. "That's why you post all those peds."

"Op-eds. But, yes, different beliefs certainly make people argue. And some people, like the Attorney General, think we should all keep our beliefs to ourselves and never say anything or act on our beliefs in public. But other people think we all should agree with everybody and celebrate what everyone believes."

Caleb shook his head. "But they believe different stuff."

"Yeah," Josh said. "If they believe different stuff, some of them gotta believe lies. Ya' can't celibate lies."

Lex grinned at Josh. "Celibate lies. Lies that can't reproduce. What an idea, Josh. That's what my news site tries to accomplish—stop the spread of lies."

"Uncalex, we wanna help. Mama and Dad would want us to help you ... until ..." Josh's voice trailed off and he swiped at an eye.

"Until we all get to be together in heaven." Caleb finished for him and then gave his brother a side hug.

"Yes, they—" Lex's voice broke. He took a deep breath and tried to give the twins a warm smile.

Josh turned his head toward his brother.

Caleb nodded. "Wono oop tap wye."

"Nonna tap wipo." Josh pursed his lips.

"Josh, Caleb, how many times have I told you it's not polite to do that in front of other people. They'll think you're talking about them. Besides, you could both use a little work on your English—celibate, fruit loops."

"But we—"

"I know you've been talking in your language since before you could walk. And you were talking about me, right?"

Caleb nodded. "But you don't know our language do ya, Uncalex?"

Josh nodded too. "But it wasn't anything bad. You're the best uncle anybody could have. If we can't have them, we want—"

The doorbell rang, ending what was becoming an intimate, painful conversation full of memories of the beautiful sister Lex had lost, the loving mother and father the boys missed, and of the injustice of a justice system that only slaps the wrists of a drunk who drives and kills people.

Lex exhaled some of the pain in a long sigh and headed toward the front door.

Please, God, don't let me fail these boys.

Chapter 4

Events of the past twenty-four hours seemed to have pushed Gemma inexorably to the door in front of her, the door to Lex James's house. There had to be a reason Gemma had been removed from WITSEC. Or was it booted out of WITSEC?

Regardless, if she was meant to play a role in unraveling the insidious conspiracy that had engulfed her ...

Please, God, show me what you want me to do.

The sounds of people talking came from inside the house.

She rang the doorbell and prepared to meet the man who seemed determined to restore integrity to journalism in the U.S.A.

No response.

Gemma raised her hand to rap hard on the door. She drove her knuckles into it but hit nothing, lost her balance, and stumbled forward through the doorway.

Strong arms caught her shoulders and stood her up. Bright blue eyes studied her. Lips just north of a chiseled chin smiled.

The man inside the door had saved Gemma from an awkward fall, otherwise, her introduction would have begun with Gemma Saint sprawled out on the floor.

"Are you okay?" He removed his hands from her shoulders.

Lex James was young, too young to have such an impact on an entire nation. And there was a lot more to what she saw, things she shouldn't even be thinking with all the problems she had.

"Uh, yes. I'm okay. And I'm sorry to barge in on you like this, but ... are you really Lex James?"

Barge in? She had fallen in. She'd really impressed Mr. Lex James.

Look at him, Gemma. He thinks you're a nutcase. Then, after you tell him why you came, you'll certify it.

"Yes, I'm Lex. I'd ask you to come in, but you've already done that."

Movement in the hallway, at the far end of the living room, caught her attention. Two boys stopped in the middle of the room. Identical twins.

Wavy blonde hair hung low on their foreheads. The look on their faces as they studied Gemma—wide-eyed and open-mouthed—lay somewhere between astonishment and awe.

Adorable faces held large, deep blue eyes that appeared wise beyond their years. When they walked it was graceful, like athletes, not like kids. The boys were, there was only one word for them ... angelic.

Gemma needed to respond to Lex, but a single look at the boys had stolen all her words. She ripped her eyes from the twins and looked at Lex. "Mr. James, they are—"

"Angelic?"

Was he psychic?

"I don't read minds, but I saw the expression on your face. We get that at church every Sunday, at the grocery store, wherever I take those two. But, as they say, looks can be deceiving."

Making gaga eyes at two four- or five-year-old boys— what must he think of her? "I didn't know you had a family. That you were married. I—I shouldn't have come." Had she actually said those words? What an idiot. What would he think?

"So if I *wasn't* married, you *should* have come? This is getting interesting." Lex gave her a teasing grin.

That grin with those words—her cheeks burned. This was no time for blushing or whatever else was happening. She could be bringing danger to this man and these boys.

One of the boys inched closer to her. "Uncalex, ask her what her name is."

"Yeah, ask her," the other boy said. "She's beeeautiful, just like mama."

Lex glanced at the boys then looked back at her. "Since I'm under orders to ask you, what's your name?"

The boys' words, their eyes ogling her, Lex's teasing that seemed to border on flirting—it seemed like her college years all over again. Pursued now by three men—one big one and two little ones. That was certainly different. To top it all off, there were no signs of *ad nauseum.*

"Well, if you'd rather not tell us ..."

"I'm sorry." She blew out a breath and tried to focus on Lex. "My name is Gemma Saint. And I think I made a mistake by coming here. But when you didn't reply to my email, and then I stumbled across your address ..."

"First things first, Ms. Saint. Please have a seat." He pointed at a long couch that curled around one corner of the living room. "And then you can tell me why you wanted to come here and why you think it was a mistake."

"Before I sit down, Mr. James—"

"Lex."

"Okay, Lex. I could be endangering you. I won't do that to you and your family. Honestly, I didn't know you were married or I wouldn't have come."

"That made a little more sense the second time. But about—"

"Uncalex? You gonna let a dangerous lady in our house?"

"Yeah. Are ya? We can get rid of her just like we—"

"Like you did the last babysitter. Josh, Caleb, go to your room until I ask you to come out. I need to hear Ms. Saint's story without your two cents."

"But we got two hundred and—"

"Caleb, that's enough. To your room now. And no spying on us with any of your contraptions."

"Aw, alright."

The two boys trudged down the hallway.

One of the twins stopped. "My squirt gun."

A plastic soaker squirt gun lay on the floor by Gemma's feet. She picked it up.

"Caleb." Lex snatched it from her and sent it spinning across the room toward the boy.

She gasped. It would hit Caleb in the face.

Caleb took a step forward and caught the gun between his two small hands.

He had the hand-eye coordination of an athletic boy two or more times his age. What other abilities did these twins have? And what did they have two-hundred of?

Gemma tried to regain her focus. They had lost time, and she might not have much of that left.

"Ms. Saint, since you came to me, I'm assuming the danger you mentioned is regarding something that's newsworthy."

She nodded. "Just call me Gemma. I'm trying to get used to using my name again."

"Your name? Did you have amnesia or something?"

"No. I'll explain in a moment. But, if I'm right, this will be the biggest story you've ever broken."

Lex's eyes darted between looking at her and out the living room window at the driveway. "Did anyone follow you here?"

"No. But they could find me at any time. And so I need to go."

"And have me pass up the biggest story I've ever broken?"

"But your boys and your wife, y'all won't—"

"Gemma, I'm not married. But you're right about the boys. I won't put them in danger. First, tell me who's after you."

"I'm not certain, but I think it's rogue or off-the-books, whatever you call them, members of the FBI."

"The FBI? You mean like a black operation?"

"Yes."

"Gemma, have you broken the law?"

"Uh ... I just got a fake ID. So, technically, I have."

"Fake ID?"

"I was in WITSEC and the FBI located me, killed the U.S. Marshal who was my inspector, and now they're after me."

"So Gemma is your real name?"

She nodded.

"I want to hear your story, but first I need to take the boys to a safe place."

"I didn't know you had any family. Honest, or I—"

"I do now. My sister and her husband were killed by a drunk driver a few months ago, and I'm the guardian for Josh and Caleb, twins, both with IQs in the vicinity of two-hundred but too high to measure at their age."

High IQs. Maybe that's why the boys seemed so different and adorable. "I'm so sorry."

"Yeah. Me and the boys too. I lost my sister and brother-in-law, but so thankful I have those two boys."

"How do you tell them apart? They're identical right down to the way their blonde hair hangs on their eyebrows."

"Mostly by their mannerisms. Josh usually leads with shock and awe. Caleb comes in behind and mows down whatever is left." Lex stood and looked out the front window where her car sat in the driveway.

Gemma stood beside him, noting the concern in his eyes.

"You need to pull your car into my garage. We'll hide it there, and you can ride with me to where I'm taking the boys. We can talk on the way. It'll save time."

"Lex, after what I've told you, would y'all rather I just left?"

Lex turned and laid his hand on her shoulder. "That's not going to happen, Gemma. What reporter in his right mind would choose to miss out on the biggest story they've ever broken? Come on. Drive your car into the garage and throw your bag in the back of my SUV, while I get the boys."

As Gemma walked to her car to park it inside Lex's garage, she still had the opportunity to leave. She could just drive away.

She turned the key to start the car, still unsure what she was going to do. But coming to his house, along with what she'd already told Lex, might bring trouble his way. That could endanger those two little angels.

If she left now, could it change that?

Chapter 5

What in the blazes was Blade up to? Max hadn't heard from him in eighteen hours. He'd had enough time to drive from Portland to Bend, find the girl, interrogate her, finish the job, and cover his trail.

And Gemma Saint, if Blade hadn't found her, had enough time to contact Lex James. Maybe the girl was smarter than they'd given her credit for.

Max's secure phone rang. The display indicated Mr. Blade Sikes. It was about time.

"Carr, here."

"It's Blade. I need to brief you on some new developments."

"Things aren't slipping out of control out west, are they?"

"No, sir. Not out of control, but the scope of this mission keeps expanding."

"Don't tell me she contacted law enforcement."

"No, sir. And if she does, we might be able to turn that to our advantage. But our little *saint* has gone *elsewhere*. Twice. But I'm—let me back up and brief you properly."

"Please do, Sikes."

"All six of us are here now. I sent three members of the team to check out Saint's apartment in Madras and to line up air support in case we need that. The two younger guys came with me to Bend."

"I take it she isn't in either place."

"We found that she stayed in a cheap motel in Bend, but she checked out at about 7:00 a.m. We think she went to the OSU-Cascades campus."

"Of course, she would go to a college campus. She needs new ID."

"Right. Like her name suggests, a saint like her wouldn't know who to contact for professional quality ID, the stuff that costs a few grand. But she did slip up at the motel. Used a burner app on her smart phone to try to contact Lex James."

"James the media mouthpiece. That's just what we need. But, before she shoots off her mouth to him, she'll have to meet with James to gain his trust and get him to cooperate."

"And that's why the three of us just pulled out onto Highway 97 headed for Terrebonne, Lex James's home. It shouldn't be much longer now. The only question is what to do with the intruder, Mr. James."

Another person who might know too much. Gemma Saint's murder could be attributed to violations in WITSEC. But danger to Carr from this operation rose exponentially with the body count. Killing Mr. James wasn't Max's preference. But, if Gemma had already briefed him ...

"He's made a lot of enemies with his investigative reporting. It would be too bad if one of them sought revenge, wouldn't it?"

Chapter 6

With Gemma beside him and the boys in the back, Lex pulled out of his dusty driveway and drove his SUV north on Southwest River Road.

It looked like Gemma had started to back out of his driveway, taking her mysterious story with her. But she stopped and pulled into his garage.

Now, Gemma stared down the highway while she chewed on a fingernail. It was the first sign of worry about her safety that Lex had seen.

Many people would be coming unglued if highly skilled government agents were coming to kill them. Seeing her composure, he and the boys being drawn to Gemma, and being completely comfortable around her—these proved that they had connected within moments of meeting. In Lex's experience, that kind of connection was usually a spiritual bond between believers.

It was worth a shot. "Gemma, are you a praying person?"

She pulled her finger from her mouth and rested her hand on the console between them. "What are you really asking me, Mr. James? Are you going to start preaching to me if I'm not?" Her coy smile tweaked the corners of her mouth.

"No. But *are* you?"

"Lex, I know about your faith. It's common knowledge because you write about it. That's part of the reason I came to you for help. You and I pray to the same Heavenly Father through the same mediator, His Son. Does that answer your question?"

"Yeah. It does." He noted the inviting hand laying palms-up on the console.

The SUV's tires thumped when they hit the reflectors on the centerline of the road. Lex, instinctively, yanked the vehicle back into the center of the lane.

Gemma gave him a strange glance that he couldn't read.

Regardless, it made him feel like the proverbial kid caught with his hand in the cookie jar. He needed to keep his eyes on the road, not on Gemma.

"How far is it to this place?"

"It's a looong, long way." Josh's voice came from the back seat.

Lex shook his head. "It's about fifteen minutes, Gemma."

"But he said—"

"When you're four, and you can't wait to see your cousin, it's an eternity."

Gemma gave him a squinty-eyed frown. "Cousin? Is that a good idea, leaving the boys with relatives. They might ..."

"They'll be fine," Lex said. "The Daniels are only shirt-tail relatives through a couple of marriages. It's not likely anyone would make the connection. Then there is that other thing ..."

"I hope it's a good thing, because I still feel like I'm—"

"It's a good thing. Don't worry about it." How should he tell her this? "Gemma, the person Josh and Caleb will be staying with is ... good with guns. Besides, it's someone no one in their right mind will mess with unless they have a death wish."

"Sounds like a modern-day gunslinger."

"Not exactly. She's KC Banning. Now KC Daniels."

"You're kidding me, right?"

Lex shook his head.

"Lex, she was my hero when I was in high school. KC and Brock both were."

"Then you realize that anyone who bothers KC would have the military, law enforcement, and three-hundred million Americans after them. A lynch party of that size will keep the boys safe." He paused. "But back to the subject at hand, Gemma Saint. How did you learn some rogue FBI agents were coming after you?"

"Marshall Cottrell's text message and then a short phone call with him—a call during which they shot him."

Lex glanced at Gemma.

The lines of stress etched on her face betrayed feelings she seemed to keep hidden most of the time.

"When and where did this happen?"

"Near Denver about thirty-six hours ago. 11:04 p.m. on the Fourth of July, to be exact."

It was enough time to fly or even drive to Central Oregon. "So they are likely in this area searching for you?"

"You can count on it." Gemma's finger went back to her mouth and her chewing resumed.

One thing could allow the danger to reach them, quickly. Lex needed to assess that likelihood. "Gemma ... is there any way they might have connected you with me?"

Gemma nodded but didn't say anything.

"I really need to know. This is important." Why was she reluctant to tell him?

"I—I emailed you last night. Well, I tried to."

"Do you mean you sent a message to the email address on my web site?"

"Yes. But, like I told you before, you didn't reply and so I got your home address and ... you know the rest."

"Yeah. I'd forgotten that you mentioned it right after you stumbled into my house."

"Too bad you didn't forget the stumbling ... and all the bumbling."

"Maybe I didn't want to forget." Had he said those words or just thought them.

Gemma looked away, out the passenger side window.

Was she blushing or angry?

Tread softly, dude. She might have a temper, or ...

Lex was hoping for *or*, but he had no business doing so. Keeping Gemma safe kept morphing into thoughts about keeping Gemma. As enticing as those thoughts were, they would only endanger her.

"Back to the email you sent."

"What about it?"

"Gemma, the FBI has a unit that intercepts Internet and cell phone communications for themselves, NSA and other government agencies."

"The FBI? I thought NSA did that."

"No, but the FBI doesn't exactly advertise that fact. It's easier to let NSA take the heat whenever a controversy arises." He paused. "But, if they found your email and used the IP addresses to see who you were contacting, they would find TAM's email server. So ..."

She looked his way. Her dark brown eyes had widened. "If they didn't find you at your office, they might come by your house."

"Exactly. After we drop off Josh and Caleb, we need to find somewhere to lay low until we decide how to use your story to protect you while we nail the bad guys."

"Exactly." Gemma looked his way and the corner of her mouth curled upward. "You wouldn't be, uh, a little like Josh and Caleb, would you?"

"No way. Uncalex don't have two hundred. But he's purty smart anyway."

"Josh, would you please keep your two hundred to yourself. Gemma and I need to talk." He steered around a sharp turn in the road, then glanced her way. "I've been accused of a lot of things, some really nasty stuff by the radical left, but never of being like Josh and Caleb."

Gemma gave him her coy smile again. "IQs of two hundred? Maybe I should be asking them for advice."

Two could play the coy game. Or was this called flirting?

If this wasn't a dangerous situation, flirting with Gemma Saint would be at the top of his to do list. "Asking Josh and Caleb for advice? Hmmm. Feel free, Gemma."

Gemma's mouth opened. But her surprised look morphed back to her coy smile. "Josh, Caleb, does your uncle have a girlfriend?"

No reply.

Gemma turned her head and looked into the back seat. "Well does he?"

"Uh ... not no more." Caleb's voice.

"Don't tell her that, Cabe. You'll scare her off." Josh had whispered the words, barely audible over the road noise.

Lex blew out a sharp sigh. "Don't tell her what? Do you mean what you two did to run off Melissa?"

Silence.

Lex waited.

"We're sorry, Uncalex."

There was a lot more to the story about Melissa, but this was not the time to tell it. Maybe he could share part of the story for Gemma's sake.

Sure, dude. All for Gemma's sake.

This was not the time for listening to obnoxious voices inside his head. "Well I'm not sorry. Melissa had her nose so high in the air she might have drowned if we lived on the other side of the mountains."

Josh and Caleb giggled and whispered.

Gemma studied Lex's face as he drove down Quail Road. She must have liked what she saw, because she was smiling too.

Lex's amygdala, or whatever they called that threat-response area of the brain had started screaming at him. There was way too much distraction here for their precarious situation.

Did Gemma realize that too? He glanced her way.

Maybe. Her smile had quickly faded.

She had a beautiful smile and the boys thought she was beautiful, like their mother.

Lex's sister was beautiful, but Gemma had a unique quality. If she walked out onto the stage at a beauty pageant, she might not be the first to catch the judges' eyes. But no matter how Lex looked at Gemma, or how he scrutinized what he saw, there wasn't a single thing about her that wasn't attractive.

Aside from the nail chewing, Gemma was as close to perfect as he'd ever seen. Well, perfect for Lex James.

However, he'd learned that looks often covered up a lot of deeper flaws inside a person, flaws that quickly detracted from outward beauty, flaws that meant you could never trust that person. Lex had a word for such flaws, *Melissa*.

He glanced at Gemma again.

She brushed what looked like a tear from one cheek.

Gemma probably had a horde of fears and insecurities waging a fierce war inside.

Enough on the enigma of Gemma Saint. Lex James needed to get his act together or he could get this woman and himself killed.

It was time to return to being the news editor of The American Motto. And time for Lex to make a vow, the same vow he had made for the boys when they came under his care.

He would die before letting anyone harm this innocent young woman.

After seeing her brushing away tears, he needed to tell Gemma that he was committed to her safety. She needed to know he was all in and would not desert her.

He would tell her as soon as he dropped off the boys at KC's house. Maybe that would stop her tears.

But how could he stop the immediate danger? Lex hadn't come up with a good plan. He shot a silent prayer heavenward and waited.

It was quiet in his SUV.

Five minutes later, still no answer.

Maybe this was one of those times that he hated, times when one simply had to trust God and wait for Him to direct a person's path. Times where Lex had to take a step into the unknown and expect that there would be a place for his next foot to come down without Lex stumbling, without Lex falling, without Lex getting Gemma Saint killed.

* * *

Gemma glanced at the street sign when they turned onto a road that skirted a cliff. Rim Road. She looked beyond the rim at the plateau below. So this was Crooked River Ranch.

In normal times, she would've gazed in awe at the green oasis of the golf course below and the miniature Grand Canyon beyond that. But the threat to her, and now to Lex, had drained away her stubborn stoicism.

Maybe Lex hadn't seen her tears, though she suspected he had. Gemma hated to show her weakness. She was not a weak person, but the last thirty-six hours had left her feeling alone and vulnerable.

Lex's hand curled around hers and held it where she had left it on the console.

Maybe she had subconsciously made it available. Regardless, strength and comfort flowed into Gemma, giving her enough of both to continue her fight for life and justice.

"Are you okay, Gemma?"

"I am now. Sometimes we need a reminder that we're not alone. Thanks."

"My pleasure."

"My pleasure? Did you put yourself through college working at Chick-fil-A?"

"No. Had a full ride swimming scholarship."

"Yeah. And Uncalex can stay underwater so long you think he's gonna drown."

Gemma shook her head. "Not me. If I go under the water, I know I'm going to drown. Gives me claustrophobia."

Lex looked her way, scanning her from the floorboard up. "You look in pretty good shape to me. What you do for exercise?"

That Lex James had just checked her out and evidently approved of what he saw, turned a swarm of butterflies loose in her stomach. She had never had that reaction to any guy. Even worse was the fact that such feelings were entirely inappropriate for someone being hunted by FBI agents.

Lex turned off the road and drove down a gravel driveway lined with juniper trees. Ahead of them, stood a two-story log house near the rim of the canyon.

"Got your squirt gun, Cabe?" Josh said. "

"Yeah. We're gonna have a squirt gun war with Benjie."

"That's fine," Lex said. "But no squirting in KC's house. And I want you to mind her. Don't give her any trouble or you'll have to answer to me when Gemma and I get back."

Josh and Caleb had a short discussion in what sounded like a foreign language. Josh leaned forward in his seat. "You hafta' bring Gemma back, Uncalex."

"So I have to?" He shook his head. "Well, you both *hafta'* mind KC."

"We'll mind," Josh said. "Aunt Kace has red hair. You don't ever wanna make her mad."

"The voice of experience." Lex looked at Gemma and grinned. "Come on let's introduce you to KC, then you and I need to get out of Dodge."

Strange relational forces seemed to be racing toward some mysterious climax. At the center, were two little geniuses who had staked a claim on Gemma Saint. But that was ridiculous. She needed to concentrate on staying alive. "Where were you thinking of hiding out, Lex?"

"Someplace where there are a lot of people and high-speed Internet access."

"Like?"

"I'm still working on that." He stopped the SUV in front of the log house.

The large wooden door swung open and a slender woman stepped out followed by a boy a year or two older than the twins.

Caleb and Josh had already unbuckled and were climbing out of the car by the time the Gemma opened her door.

The boys ran to meet their cousin and the three disappeared through the front door.

Gemma followed Lex to the porch where KC stood.

"Thanks, KC. I owe you a big one." He turned toward Gemma. "This is Gemma Saint."

Gemma offered her hand.

KC took it but held onto it. "Good to meet you, Gemma. I've been reading about you since Lex called me. After Marshall McDowell's trial, all mention of you stops."

"That's when I entered witness protection."

"So the DOJ used you, then put you in WITSEC? It doesn't make sense. I think there's a dead skunk in the RFK Building ... or maybe across the street."

Gemma nodded. "And that's an odor you would be familiar with."

KC grinned but it soon disappeared. She squeezed Gemma's hand then released it. "I'll be praying for you two. Brock will too, as soon as I can reach him. He's on a road trip until the All-Star Game."

"I hope the odor back there doesn't affect his pitching," Lex said

"Me too," KC said. "Nationals Park isn't that far away from the Capitol. I decided to stay home with Benjie this year. It's a long trip and we don't even know if Brock will get to close."

"We need to go. We'll contact you at this e-mail address." Lex handed KC a slip of paper. "It's an account I had set up for me to communicate with informants who want to remain anonymous. My messages will be in the draft folder. You can edit the draft to respond."

"Got it. And I'll take good care of the boys. They'll be occupied, playing with Benjie. You take care too."

Gemma's gaze met KC's and locked there. The transaction between them completed in that moment, a transaction of mutual concern and understanding. KC had been where Gemma now stood, with a corrupt and powerful person wanting to eliminate her.

KC knew the fear and the uncertainty of looking at her future and seeing only question marks.

Gemma gave KC a quick hug.

Lex hooked Gemma's arm and they strode back to the SUV, while giggles and high-pitched squeals of little boys sounded from the open door.

Lex and Gemma buckled in. He turned the SUV around and headed down the driveway toward Rim Road.

"She's beautiful, Lex. With all that red hair and freckles, she looks like an Irish princess."

Lex stopped at the end of the driveway and checked for traffic. "Yeah. Brock's a lucky man. Guess I should say blessed. Wish I could be blessed like that." Lex looked her way and didn't stop looking until she met his intense gaze.

Gemma's face hit flashpoint. Her cheeks burned. Why would Lex say something like that? She looked away, out the passenger-side window.

Lex seemed to enjoy teasing. And he'd grinned when he did that. But there had been no grin this time. He seemed dead serious and he wanted her to know it.

So what do you plan to do about that, Gemma Saint?

She hadn't a clue. And the question might be moot, because Gemma Saint might not be alive at the end of this day.

Chapter 7

Lex pulled out onto Rim Road headed for Terrebonne.

He had embarrassed Gemma. He had said more than he intended to say, but not even half of what he felt. Should he even be having such thoughts and feelings about someone he'd only known for a couple of hours?

Probably not. But he had a reason. Gemma was a damsel in distress, and he was the knight coming to save her. That was the fairytale version of the story and maybe it was part of the attraction.

In reality, he was likely the best-suited person on the planet to end the danger to her by breaking her story, along with all of its supporting facts. But was he the best man to keep her alive until that time? The answer to that question haunted him.

Lex glanced at her long, dark hair.

Her large brown eyes responded by looking at him.

"Gemma, are you Italian?"

"How'd you—are you from Jersey?"

"No. But despite the Texas drawl, your name and ... uh, features are rather Italian."

"I'm half Italian. My mom's folks came from Italy. I was born in New Jersey. Dad taught at Princeton, until we moved to Texas. But, after twelve years in Texas, people down there think mom's Hispanic. Some think I am too."

"Where is 'down there'?"

"College Station, home of the Fightin' Texas Aggies."

"Is that where you went to school?"

"Well, I sure didn't go back to Princeton. Dad didn't— that's probably more than you wanted to know. Now that you know all about me, what about Lex James?"

All about Gemma Saint. He hoped he'd get that chance. "Lex James ... he's a boring guy."

"Lighting up the media across America, upsetting the political applecart, guardian to genius twins—y'all ... uh, you guys are anything but boring.

"You don't need to forget Texas on my account."

"No. I need ... uh, needed to do that on my account. So nobody could connect me to my former life." She gave him a warm smile. "Y'all gonna tell me about Lex James, or not? Where did you go to school?"

"Washington State. Studied journalism and media production on a swimming scholarship. Do you swim?"

"I can stay afloat. Does that qualify?"

"Yeah. If you can actually move through the water."

Gemma gave him that irresistible smile that lit up her face and everything around her.

The talking stopped and it grew quiet in the car.

They rounded a turn and Lex slowed the SUV as they approached the intersection with Chinook Drive.

A black van sat at the stop sign. It hadn't moved since it came into view ten or fifteen seconds ago.

A tingling sensation ran up the back of Lex's neck. He needed to lose that van.

"Gemma, the black van could be trouble. Look for any sign of—"

The van pulled forward, then stopped, blocking southbound Chinook Drive at the T in front of them.

Lex steered into the left lane. "Hang on, Gemma."

He yanked the wheel hard left and turned onto Chinook Drive, northbound.

"Two men got out. Lex, they have guns!"

Lex mashed the accelerator to the floor and used his right hand to shove Gemma's head down to the seat.

The tat, tat, tat of automatic weapon fire sounded.

The rear window of Lex's SUV exploded.

Glass particles pelted the interior.

"Stay down, Gemma." He had to pull his right hand from her head to steer.

His SUV fishtailed down the road as the powerful engine spun the squealing tires.

The shooting stopped.

Lex glanced in the rearview mirror.

The men were gone, but the van had backed up, preparing to turn their way.

Gemma sat up in her seat. "It's them." Her words came out in a hoarse whisper, barely audible above the roaring engine. "I'll watch them, Lex. You just lose them."

Lex accelerated to triple the speed limit as they rocketed past the entrance to the Crooked River Ranch Golf Course. "Lose them? That's going to be a problem."

"What do you mean? Your SUV seems to have a lot of power."

"It does. But the direction we're headed—in about three miles the road dead ends at Otter Bench Trail."

"Isn't there any other road we can turn onto?" Desperation had crept into Gemma's voice.

He had never heard it before, and it ripped through his heart like a dull knife. "The only road turns back the other way in a hairpin turn. If I slowed to take it, we'd be doubling back alongside them."

"What's at that Otter Bench place?"

"That depends." Lex shoved the accelerator to the floor as he entered a straight stretch, then he glanced at those sleek but athletic-looking legs beside him. "Did you run track in high school?"

"No. Cross country."

"That's even better. What kind of shape are you in?" Lex looked her way, then shook his head and mumbled, "Stupid question."

Gemma shot him a sharp glance. "You need to keep your head in the game, Lex."

"That was supposed to be my line."

"I can run, if that's what you meant."

"Hold on." Lex braked hard, then accelerated out of the turn. "We're opening up a little lead. Our only chance is to get at least a quarter mile ahead of them, stop at the trail head, and run down the trail. We'll have a big lead, but we've got to maintain it or ..."

"Yeah, or ... But Lex, it's almost noon and it's probably ninety-five degrees out there, headed for one hundred."

"That's why I asked if you were in good shape."

"That's not quite how you put it."

"Listen, Gemma, these guys are cops, FBI. They'll be in pretty good shape. But I'd bet my life they can't run five miles in this heat and catch us if we have a quarter-mile lead. Are you willing to bet yours?"

Gemma's hand clamped onto his shoulder and squeezed. Her strength surprised him.

Lex looked at her, trying to see the source of that strength.

An intensity burned in Gemma's brown eyes that he'd never seen before.

She nodded. "I can do this, Lex. How about you?"

He dipped his head, then studied the road. "As long as neither of us sprains an ankle or something, we're good to go."

Gemma squeezed his shoulder again. "You said we had to run five miles. What's five miles down the trail?"

Lex cleared his throat. "Uh ..."

"Well?"

"Lake Billy Chinook."

"Lex, I told you about me and water. I get—"

"Gemma, let me worry about the lake. You just get ready to run."

Chapter 8

Lex pushed the gas pedal to the floor.

His SUV responded and they flew down the dirt road at an insane speed.

"Get ready. We're coming to the loop at the trail head." He tapped the brakes. "When I stop, push open your door and run hard down the trail. It's level and smooth for the first half mile or so."

"My purse is here. Should I bring—"

"Don't bring anything that slows you down."

She shoved her purse under the seat. "But, Lex, the land is flat here. Can't they just keep driving and run us down?"

"No vehicles are allowed on the trail. They've fenced it off with big rocks and a steel gate. Only people and bicycles can get through."

He circled a small cluster of juniper trees and stomped on the brake pedal.

The SUV slid sideways and stopped in a swirling cloud of gray-brown dust. The passenger-side door ended up even with the gate.

By the time Lex got out and circled his vehicle, Gemma was flying down the trail at an incredible rate.

Dude, she can run!

For once Lex agreed with the obnoxious voice inside. But, the question was, would Lex catch her or collapse first? On the positive side, if Lex couldn't catch her, neither could the gunmen.

The dusty trail ran nearly straight for a quarter mile through a desert of sparse, dry bunch grass dotted with juniper trees. Beyond that it appeared to veer to the right.

If they could keep enough trees between them and their pursuers, there should be no more shooting, and the guys chasing them wouldn't see it when they veered off onto the Pink Trail in about two more miles.

Lex usually ran, or performed other workouts, three or four times a week. It had been more before he got the twins. However, sprinting was never part of his workout.

He gradually coaxed his legs up to a full sprint, hoping the hundred-degree temperature would prevent him from pulling any muscles.

A hundred yards down the trail, breathing like a snorting racehorse in the final stretch, Lex opened up his stride. He pumped hard with his arms.

But Gemma's flawless running style, smooth and effortless looking, was running him into the ground.

He had gained only a few yards on her.

To get away safely, they needed to be together, communicating.

Lex reached deeper and found a little more energy and speed.

His heart thumped against his sternum like a ball-peen hammer, but he had gained on Gemma.

They were over a quarter mile down the trail when Lex looked back at the trailhead, just before the juniper trees blocked his view of it.

Their pursuers van slid to a stop.

Three men jumped from the van.

A bend in the trail took the van out of Lex's view.

The men would follow. Of that he was sure.

Now, the trail veered toward the canyon.

Soon, four hundred feet below them, a blue ribbon of water came into view, meandering through the canyon, Crooked River.

Lex's shirt grew damp. That was an understatement. He could wring water out of it. Sweat poured off his forehead. In these temperatures, if they couldn't find drinking water soon, dehydration could become a life-threatening problem.

Now, twenty yards behind Gemma, Lex was eating the dust her flying feet kicked up.

With his lungs burning and his legs feeling like they had been manufactured by Goodyear, Lex reached Gemma's side. "Slow ... it down ... a bit."

Gemma slowed, but not enough.

Lex glanced back down the trail.

In the far distance, a lone figure ran their way.

Lex ran another hundred yards, then turned and looked back again, before the juniper trees cut off his view.

The runner seemed to be slowing.

They could do this. He and Gemma could run these guys into the ground and get away ... for now. That confidence sent endorphins and adrenaline surging through Lex's body.

He sped up and moved to Gemma's side. "I ... think they're ... giving up."

She looked his way. "They won't ... do that. Not permanently." Heavy breaths chopped apart her words.

If Gemma could keep up this pace in temperatures approaching one-hundred degrees, the men in the van would probably give up the chase and try to catch Lex and Gemma later, after they left this desolate area.

For now, Lex's job was to keep the bad dudes guessing and offer no clues as to where he and Gemma might emerge.

Lex had no clue where that would be. Nor did he know how he would get the water they needed to survive. He knew of one location downriver with drinkable water, but how could they reach it without being caught, or dehydrating?

Then there was the question of sniper rifles. If these dudes had one, and if they followed far enough, they could pick off Gemma and him when Pink Trail doubled back to the south where it descended into the gorge.

Despite leaving the gunmen in the dust, he and Gemma were still in deep water.

The trail now skirted the edge of the canyon. With sweat pouring off Lex's forehead and stinging his eyes, the water of the Crooked River, four hundred feet below, looked inviting.

Gemma's gaze seemed to be following the river too. She glanced back at him, "Lex ... we're going to need water soon ... can we drink from the river?"

"Just keep running, Gemma. We've got to *make* it to the river ... before we think about drinking from it."

"Speak ... for yourself ... it's all I can think about ... water."

"Then think about this ... if they have sniper rifles ... they can kill us from a thousand yards."

"Just tell me I can drink from the river ... and I'll get us there more than a thousand yards ahead of them."

"Gemma ... that river flows over a hundred miles through the desert ... and some farmland ... probably full of little parasites ... the kind that make you puke and the other stuff too ... it would force us to go for medical help."

"How far to ... that Pink Trail?"

"Almost there and ... we get to slow down."

"Why?"

"Steep."

"Look at that canyon ... it's a four-hundred-foot vertical drop ... is this trail ... climbing-gear steep?"

"No. Steep as in we won't be running ... so we need to keep our lead. And Gem you need ..."

"Don't do that, Lex!" She shot him a sharp glance.

"Don't do what?"

"Shorten my name to Gem ... sounds like a guy's name. ... I hate that."

"Not to worry ... from back here nobody's going to mistake *you* for a guy."

"Great! ... We're being chased by gunmen ... and all you can think about is—"

"Well, it's better than thinking about bullets."

She didn't reply.

They'd almost run by the Pink Trail. "Go right, Gemma. And slow down ... time to become mountain goats ... we can't afford a fall."

She didn't slow down. Gemma plunged over the break and ran down the Pink Trail.

"Come on, Gemma! Slow down!"

"Can't. Look below ... trail doubles back ... we'll be running back toward them and those sniper rifles ... they'll shoot us from the rim." Gemma slowed, but still ran faster than a jog.

This pace was easier, and they were running downhill. Lex was catching his breath but running on rubbery legs.

He hadn't seen any signs of their pursuers for the last half mile. "Gemma ... know what I think?"

Gemma slowed as the trail grew rockier. She glanced back at him. "You already told me what you think, *Lech.*"

"You mean Lex."

"Not after what you said. This is the last time I let you run behind me."

"Let's just hope it's not the last time we run, period."

Gemma's foot came down on a patch of pebbles. Her foot slid, throwing her off balance, headed for a rear-end landing.

Lex drew a sharp breath when he saw the cliff on the right, a one-hundred-foot drop to a rocky bench below.

Gemma's body tilted toward the cliff as she fell.

He lurched forward and scooped her upper body before it hit the ground.

Lex pulled her against his chest and leaned backward digging his heels into the gravel and dirt of the trail. He stumbled to his right. Somehow, he managed to bring them both to a stop ... five feet from the drop-off.

He'd prevented a nasty fall, maybe a deadly one if they had lost their balance and fallen to their right. But, in his panic to stop her fall, Lex had grabbed Gemma in a way that, under most circumstances, would be highly inappropriate.

He quickly moved his hands under her arms and lifted her to standing position, while the cloud of dust they had generated swirled around them.

The dust flew off to the south carried by the growing breeze.

Lex managed to catch his breath. "Are you okay?"

Gemma turned to face him.

He held her shoulders and studied her face.

The weird look in her eyes quickly morphed to Gemma's intense, data-gathering look. Her gaze met his. "I'm okay ... Lech."

Lex's face heated several degrees beyond what their nearly two-mile run in one-hundred-degree temperature could produce. "I didn't mean to, you know ... I was only trying to—"

"I forgive you, Lech." One corner of her mouth edged upward. Then Gemma turned to resume their run.

She froze. Her eyes locked on the cliff that had snuck up on them hardly five feet away. She gasped, leaned back into Lex, and her breathing turned to panting.

He wrapped her up in his arms and held her. "You're safe. But you need to be more careful. And I think our gunmen have stopped chasing us, for now. You helped me outrun them."

After several seconds, Gemma's breathing returned to normal, but she continued leaning against him. She relaxed and laid the back of her head on his shoulder.

They both dripped with perspiration.

Lex could probably wring it out of his shirt.

Wet tresses of hair stuck to her forehead.

But Gemma's face lay on his shoulder for the first time only inches away.

Sweat he could deal with. So the question became should he or should he not?

Gemma didn't seem in a hurry to move. Was that an invitation? Surely not with gunmen a mile behind them.

Lex was deeply drawn to this young woman. There was no denying that. Everything he had observed said the attraction was mutual.

The answer Lex settled on was, sorta'.

He cupped her cheek and kissed her sweaty forehead. Salty but sweet. And, like everything about Gemma that he had evaluated, perfect for Lex James.

"Come on, Gem. We could both use a dip in the river to cool down."

She raised her head and turned to face him, remaining much closer than necessary. "You passed the test." Her words came wrapped in a hoarse whisper.

"So I can call you Gem?"

"Only in private."

"And you'll stop calling me—"

She pressed a finger over his lips, muting his words. "Race you to the river, Lex."

Chapter 9

Bladen Sikes sat in his rented van at the Otter Bench trail head cursing at the SUV sitting in front of him, doors open, occupants who knows where.

If his team didn't take care of the two newsmongers soon, somebody's head would roll, and it wasn't going to be Blade's.

Where was Kirby and his favorite play toy, the GA Precision rifle that he ran down the trail with? He hit Kirby's number on his sat phone.

"Kirby here."

"This is Blade. Haven't you ran those two down yet?"

"You gotta be kidding. That girl should be on the U.S. Olympic team."

"That is not what I expected to hear, commentary on the athletic abilities of our little saint."

"She may be slender, but she outran James and me."

"So you got James?"

"I didn't' say that."

"Come on, Kirby. You didn't need to *run* them down, just *gun* them down. And you can do that even if they have a thousand yards on you."

"They actually had more than that. I'd swear Gemma Saint flew down that trail. And there are just enough juniper trees to block line-of-sight for that distance. But I know where they are. I think you need to call for the chopper."

"If I need to. Now tell me why I need to. The maps say this bench ends in about four or five miles, and it's a sheer five-hundred-foot drop down to the river, higher in some places. They're trapped."

"No, Blade. There's a trail that goes down to the river."

"Sure there is. These two didn't exactly have ropes and carabiners hanging off them when they left the SUV."

"It's called the Pink Trail. I didn't try it, but evidently some people do. It's the only way they could have gotten away."

"So they're in the canyon?"

"I'm sure of it."

"Okay, I'll call for Drake and the chopper crew. We need to find them before dark, so we can end this little game of hide and seek."

"Blade, do you plan to fly over them and shoot them from the chopper?"

"You got any other ideas?"

"Well, if you look around this area, you can't go more than a half mile without running into some kind of house. I can't see why, but people actually live in this desert."

"Look, we take them out and we disappear. This whole operation is off-the-books. It never happened, and we didn't do it if it did. Carr will back us up. After all, this was his brainstorm."

"Do you want me to wait here and watch the canyon until the chopper arrives? You know, so they don't backtrack?"

"It might be two hours, or more. Do you enjoy the heat, Kirby?"

"I've got water."

"Walker and I have the air-conditioned van. Okay, you watch the canyon until 2:30, then come back and we'll drive around to where these two are going to come out of the canyon."

Kirby swore. "If you know where they're going, why do I have to stay here and bake in this sun?"

"If they happen to backtrack, maybe to get James's car, I want you there to take them out with your *precision* shooting."

Blade ended the call.

How could a slip of a girl with a name like Saint and a would-be journalist cause so much trouble? And why couldn't the best agents the FBI had run them down and gun them down?

As long as they eliminated the two before this ended, Blade wouldn't have to answer any potentially embarrassing questions from Carr tomorrow morning.

Gemma Saint seemed to have led a charmed life up until now. She was always one small step ahead. But, if Blade had calculated correctly, her charm would soon disappear.

Chapter 10

Pink Trail ended at river level on a flat, rocky bench. Patches of bushes and scrubby trees grew between the rocks. But this meager vegetation would hardly hide their bodies and would not stop bullets.

Twenty-five yards ahead of Lex and Gemma, the river ran strong and the current accelerated toward the rapids below. Maybe they couldn't drink from the river but soaking in its chilly water would cool their over-heated bodies.

The air at the bottom of the canyon became an oven in the searing afternoon sun, and the afternoon wind blew up river, dry and hot. Rather than refreshing them, the breeze sucked more moisture from them.

Lex pulled Gemma to a stop at the edge of the river.

Something wasn't right. A tingling up the back of his neck seemed to confirm it.

He scanned the rim looming above them, looking for movement. Nothing. Then he surveyed the rocks and vegetation for protection.

Twenty feet down river from Lex, a rock shattered and sprayed fragments into the stream. From up river, a crack sounded, reverberating between the canyon walls.

"Sniper!" He hooked Gemma's arm and dove behind a three-foot-high rock. "Keep your head down. His first shot was high, because he's shooting downhill. The second one won't be."

She pressed her head against his shoulder. "Could— could you tell where he was?"

"Sounded like he was way up river, but with all the echoing ..."

"So now what?"

"We've got to get out of here. If we let him keep us pinned down, he'll move along the rim until he's on top of us. At some point, the rocks won't provide cover and ..."

"Don't say it, Lex. We've come too far. God wouldn't let that happen."

"He doesn't always stop the bad things, Gemma. Like drunk drivers from killing people you love."

"You are really encouraging. Did you know that? Don't answer. I'm praying anyway."

"I didn't say don't pray. It's just that—never mind. I've got to locate all the rocks that we can use for cover if we move downstream."

She grabbed his arm. "But he can move toward us faster than we can go from rock to rock. We need a better plan."

"The river's not deep enough for us to swim underwater. You need seven or eight feet of water to stop bullets."

"I couldn't stand being under for more than a few seconds anyway."

"Even if someone was shooting at you?"

She didn't reply.

Rocks clattered down the cliff and splashed into the river.

"I hope that was him falling off the rim," Gemma said.

Lex peered around the corner of the rock they lay behind. He pulled his hand from the rock when it scorched his right hand. "No such luck. Just some rocks falling. He probably knocked them loose."

Dust from the rocks swirled in the wind and then blew up river.

Based on the rocks he had knocked loose, the sniper appeared to be about a thousand yards upstream. At that distance, his shots would be accurate. And, if he got within

52

five-hundred yards, the small boulder wouldn't protect their entire bodies. The sniper could shoot directly down on them.

"Gemma, in a couple of minutes he's going to be nearly on top of us."

"We need to do something. I'm not going to lay here with my head against a hot rock while he shoots my legs off."

"That's about the size of it."

"What do you mean?"

"I don't know what I mean, Gemma." Lex blew out a blast of air.

This situation had hopeless tattooed all over it. Maybe he should start thinking about how to sacrifice himself to save Gemma. She was the one who needed stay alive if justice was going to be served.

But what about the boys? They needed him, right now. He was Josh and Caleb's stability and their link to their parents.

Lex stopped breathing when a loud buzzing echoed through the canyon.

Gemma's wide eyes looked up into his. "Is that some kind of alarm?"

"You could say that. It's called an alarmed rattlesnake, and this one sounds really riled."

From the rim a yell sounded. Or was it a scream?

The buzzing continued.

Another gunshot echoed through the canyon.

The buzzing stopped.

A groan sounded from the canyon rim.

"Lex, was that what I think it was?"

"It was one rattlesnake fighting another. The wrong snake won but, if I'm correctly interpreting what I heard, we just leased another chunk of life." Lex jumped up, pulling Gemma with him. "Run into the river and swim downstream as fast as you can."

"But, Lex—"

"Just do it. We'll go down river while the sniper is trying to decide what to do about those two holes in his leg and the snake venom running through his bloodstream."

Hand-in-hand they plunged into the swift current of the river.

When the water ripped at Lex's thighs, he took the plunge and pulled Gemma down beside him in the chilling water.

"Swim hard until we get around the bend. I'll find a boulder we can hide behind and rest."

He pushed Gemma downstream ahead of him.

She pawed and kicked at the water. It wasn't an efficient stroke, but with the aid of the current, they were putting lifesaving distance between them and the sniper.

If only the snake bite would keep him distracted for a couple minutes more.

When they entered the rapids below Pink Trail, Lex pulled hard on the water until he maneuvered his body downstream of Gemma. He guided her through the rocks jutting up from the river bottom.

Gemma was a quick thinker. Without being told, she entered the rapids with her feet downstream. One crack of their heads against a rock would be as deadly as the sniper.

They shot through the rapids and rounded the bend. When the water smoothed and deepened, Lex raised his head and looked downstream. He did a double take.

He could see all the way to the Opal Springs Dam, maybe a half mile down the river.

Lex turned to his left and studied the canyon on the west side of the river. A short way downriver the cliff on the west side became a giant stairstep. The step, a bench about a hundred yards wide, would push the gunmen back more than a hundred yards from the base of the canyon.

If he and Gemma hugged the west bank of the river, there would be no more shots from the rim. The sniper couldn't see them.

With the tension of the previous hour easing, Lex took Gemma's hand and pulled her to the left bank of the river. "He can't see us now. Let's drift and rest a while."

Gemma nodded. "Lex, can I take a drink from the river? Just one? Please?"

"If you promise you won't swallow, you can rinse your mouth out, but be sure to spit it all out."

He pointed to the line across the river about a half-mile away. "See the dam?"

When she didn't reply, Lex looked back.

Gemma was floating on her back, spouting water from her mouth.

"You look like a whale." Not her slender, shapely body, just the spout. Maybe he should have qualified his statement.

Her head rose from the water and she gave him a serious frown. "Gee, thanks."

"I meant your mouth."

"Have you ever looked at a whale's mouth? Gross, Lex. It's really gross."

Unlike Gemma's mouth. Unlike anything related to Gemma. But this wasn't the time for these kinds of thoughts. "How are you doing? Can you tread water and maybe swim a little for another ten minutes?"

"I can do that. It's amazing how being in the water tricks you into thinking you're not as thirsty."

"It cools us off so our bodies don't need water as badly."

Lex snagged Gemma's hand and pulled her close to him.

"Lex, what are you doing?"

Treading water, they could stay afloat with an occasional kick of their legs and a wave of their hands. He spoke in hushed tones barely audible above the sound of the rushing water. "We need to talk, but we don't need our voices echoing through the canyon."

"Talk about what?"

"The dam's about a half mile below us. It's a small hydro project. And it's also where they get that Earth2O water, the same water you got from your tap in Madras."

"You've got to be kidding. I was drinking two-dollar-a-bottle, tree-hugger's water from my tap? I should have started my own business. But you are saying there's drinking water ahead?"

"Yes. But we're going to have to sneak past the security people at the dam. We'll do that after dark."

"But that's not until after 10:00 p.m."

"That's right. About nine hours from now."

"Nine hours? I think I'll get a drink now. The river looks clear enough."

"When you start puking and doing other stuff, don't ask me to help."

"I won't."

"You won't what?"

She blew out a sigh of defeat. "I won't take a drink."

"Good girl."

"Is that how you think of me?" Her eyes widened. "Never mind. Pretend I didn't say that. So what do we do for nine hours?"

"We'll hide behind the rocks on the west side of the river, somewhere just above the dam. No one can see us unless they float down the river or ..."

"Or what?"

"Come after us in a chopper."

* * *

Lex's sport watch had survived the time in the water. It said 2:30 p.m. when he helped Gemma out of the water and into the shelter of the rocks on the west bank of the river.

The dam lay less than two-hundred yards below them.

He'd found a tiny cove behind a rock formation tucked against the vertical cliff. The surrounding rocks would hide them unless their pursuers flew directly over them—not likely if a pilot wanted his wings or the rotor to avoid the rock cliff. And Lex doubted anyone would swim into the cove as he and Gemma had done.

The sun couldn't reach this part of the canyon in the afternoon. And, after spending well over an hour in the cold water, Lex's lips had turned blue.

Gemma shivered while she tried to give herself a bear hug.

It had been a grueling run and probably a frightening trip down the river for Gemma. But they were safe until tonight. Lex needed to lighten things up. "Gem, if you fattened up a bit you wouldn't have that shivering problem."

"Fattened up? You already called me a whale."

"Come here." He scooted to Gemma's side on the flat rock serving as their bench.

"What are you up to, Lex James?" She snuggled against him.

He'd noticed a pattern. Gemma's words and behavior often didn't match. What she said could seem harsh and unfriendly, but what Gemma *did* was often completely contradictory. It was much friendlier. At times, it became intimate. At least that's how she'd behaved around Lex.

Gemma probably had a lot of trust issues. That can happen when the DOJ says they're giving you protection then sets you up to take you out. Maybe her difficulty in trusting people made her reluctant to acknowledge their obvious mutual attraction.

Gemma's body, trembling against his, felt like an earthquake. Maybe a four or five on the Richter scale.

"What am I up to? Gemma, you've got a mild case of hypothermia. Me too."

"I can't believe we've got hypothermia with the temperature nearly a hundred degrees."

Lex wrapped her up in his arms and rubbed the goosebumps on hers. "Don't worry. It won't last long at these temperatures."

"This is rather—do you do this on a regular basis?" One corner of Gemma's mouth lifted. Her enigmatic smile.

"Only with people I like. Other hypothermiacs can just shake, rattle and roll."

"Lex, was Melissa one of those people you liked?"

Where was this going? "She was a friend, a girl I've known since grade school."

"But did you *like* her?" She put a strong emphasis on like.

"I don't know. That's what I was trying to find out. We were friends. Did a few things together, usually with a group from church. Then Josh and Caleb came into my life."

"And they ran her off?" Gemma studied his face.

"That's their version. A little melodramatic. From the time I got them, I knew the boys would need more than just me. They were going to need a mother as soon as they were through grieving."

"Where are they with that?"

"Crossing the finish line." They seemed to be handling it better than Lex. "Those two are amazing. So bright, yet so much faith. They'll be fine. But right after I brought the twins home, Melissa did an about-face. I saw a side of her I'd never seen before. One I didn't like."

"Sorry I brought this up. You don't have to talk about it if—"

"No. It's okay, Gemma." He looked down into her eyes, deep brown pools that, in a strange way, reminded him of looking into Josh and Caleb's eyes. But his heart didn't thump like this when he looked at the boys, unless they had gotten into serious mischief.

With Gemma pressed tightly against him, she could probably feel each thump?

Lex sighed. "Disloyalty and lack of commitment ... probably the two biggest failings of human beings. Melissa had them both."

People always seemed to let him down. He couldn't trust them. Melissa wasn't the exception, she just happened to be the most hurtful betrayal, and it came at a critical juncture in Lex's life.

That's when he had decided to stop looking for a new mom for the twins. Then Gemma came into the picture and, in a few hours, everything seemed to have changed ... provided their flight from the gunmen had a happy ending. And provided Lex wasn't being overly presumptuous.

* * *

Gemma replayed Lex's words. He had said he saw serious defects in Melissa. And he had said he didn't mind talking about her.

So, should she cast some bait on the waters? Silly question. "Lex, does that mean you didn't really love her?"

"Gemma, I could never love a woman like her. Besides, love is more than just a bunch of feelings."

Lex had set himself up for this question. "Love without feelings? So what does love mean to *you*?"

Girl, why are you asking him that? That's dangerous ground. You're jinxed, Gemma. Bad luck. You hurt people.

Gemma tried to choke the life out of the accusing voice inside. Besides, she only wanted to know his perspective on love. That's all. To file it away for ... whatever.

"I wasn't implying there are no feelings. But my definition of love. Okay. Suppose I was attracted to you, Gemma."

She drew a sharp breath. Her arms were still around Lex to soak in his warmth. She was doing plenty of that.

Maybe this conversation wasn't a good idea.

Lex continued. "You know what I mean, really attracted to you. I just can't get you out of my mind. It's to the point where I want to spend every waking minute with you. My heart does that skip-a-beat thing every time you're near. And the thought of kissing you drives me completely—"

"That's enough." Gemma's heart was doing double time and Lex could probably feel it as tightly as they were wound around each other. "I—I get the idea."

"No, you don't. Listen. Suppose all those things were true about my feelings for you. Those are still just feelings. Only when I give my heart to you, unreservedly, committing it always and forever to you, do all those feelings have a meaningful context. My commitment validates them, makes it all part of my love for you. Now, I truly love you, because out of all the women on the planet, I have chosen you and you alone."

"But all this is hypothetical, right?" Had she actually said that? Maybe she had only thought it. Her mind was in such a muddle after hearing Lex pour out his heart to her … well, hypothetically.

Lex's soliloquy continued, so maybe he hadn't heard her. "But before the commitment, before I chose you, it was only feelings.

"You mean chemistry?" Her voice had gone hoarse and it cracked on the last word.

"Yes. But chemicals get used up. Chemical reactions end and batteries go dead. You need something to keep them charged, something to sustain a relationship."

"Lex, marriages break up every day. What do you do when feelings change? And what do you do if I—if a person causes bad things to happen to you? If they always bring bad luck?"

She had to ask. Would Lex abandon her when the bad things started happening like they always did? Gemma's jinx?

"Of course, things change over time. But, if I was committed to love the person I chose, there would always be new feelings brought by new aspects of the relationship."

Lex had changed back to first person.

"Gemma, it's just like God says. Love always protects, always trusts, always hopes, always perseveres ... love never fails."

It felt like Lex was talking to her. He must be.

I need him to be.

After being alone for the past eight months, Gemma didn't want that kind of life for another month or even another minute.

Maybe, if she set her mind to it, she could do something right and not bring calamity on the people she cared about, people like Lex.

He had stopped talking.

When had that happened? She didn't know. But she did know Gemma Saint was warm now ... warmer than warm. And breathing a little too hard for a body at rest.

Lex felt warm too. But they were still holding on to each other like two—that simile wasn't going where she intended.

Hypothermia was over. Hyperventilation on the other hand ...

Gemma looked out of the cove toward the river.

With the canyon now enveloped in shadows, twilight had begun in Crooked River Canyon.

Lex's arms tightened around her. He had stopped breathing.

Evidently, hyperventilation was over too. Something had changed.

Gemma pulled her cheek from the comfortable, comforting place where it had rested, his chest, and she listened.

Within a few seconds, she understood.

In the distance, the wop, wop, wop of a helicopter's rotor sounded.

The menacing noise grew louder.

Chapter 11

Lex released Gemma when she tried to sit up. Evidently, she had heard the chopper too.

He looked up river toward the noise. His heart went from a trot to a gallop. "It's coming down the river and it's down in the canyon."

Gemma's body stiffened. "They will see us."

"Maybe not if we move to the other side of the cove. They can't see us there unless they look behind them, after passing over us. But your red shorts and white tank top—"

"Yeah. I'm a neon sign."

"Not if I cover you up. At least I'm wearing shades of brown. Come on, we need to snuggle again. Aren't you excited?"

"Y'all ain't funny, Lex James." She crawled to the other side of the tiny cove and pressed her body against the rock.

"Maybe not all of me. But part of you is."

"Now you're making fun of the way I talk."

"So talk like, who was it, Georgia Simpson?"

"I buried her and celebrated two days ago."

Lex laid against Gemma, covering her bright clothing with his. "Have I got you covered?"

The helicopter's engine grew deafening as it echoed off the canyon walls.

"This is not ladylike, Lex."

"I love the alliteration, but that's not what I asked."

"Yeah. I'm covered."

"Here they come. Don't move."

The chopper inched its way down the canyon.

Lex couldn't see it well from his position at the base of the rock. If shooting started, he needed to react, instantly, or they had no chance to survive an attack. But covering Gemma, he could barely see the chopper. He only had one option.

Please, God, don't let them start shooting.

The helicopter stopped near them, then slowly swung around in a full three-sixty, as if this location was suspect.

Lex willed the helicopter to move downriver.

It didn't. The chopper hovered, in place. Hardly fifty yards away.

"What's happening?" Gemma squirmed beneath him.

"They stopped, almost over us. Stop your squirming"

"If they start poking out guns, you've got to let me know, Lex."

"Why?"

"Because I—I've got to—"

"It's climbing, Gemma." He blew out his relief in a single blast of air.

The helicopter slowly rose out of the Canyon.

Lex looked down at Gemma's face. "What were you saying?"

"It—it doesn't matter."

"Maybe it does to me. Why did you want me to tell you if the guns—"

She pushed Lex off from her and sat up. "Because—did anyone ever tell you that you're a little slow?"

"The twins say that all the time."

"Lex ..." Gemma clasped her hands behind his neck and pulled.

He didn't resist.

Gemma was stronger than she looked. He might not have been able to prevent what was coming. Not that he wanted to, anyway.

Her huge brown eyes blurred as they moved within inches of his. "I didn't want to go through everything we've been through and then get shot to death before ... before ..."

Gemma kissed him.

Like everything else about Gemma, it was perfect ... well, perfect for Lex James.

The past four hours, culminating in Gemma's kiss, had awakened something in Lex for the first time. What should he say? What should he not say?

He fumbled for words until Gemma's penetrating gaze jarred the words loose, a verbal fumble. "You didn't have to force me to do that. You could've asked."

"Forced? You didn't put up much resistance, Lex. Besides, I would never beg anyone for a kiss."

Gemma may not realize it but, at the moment, she was begging for one. And Lex would have obliged her, but he needed to see what the chopper was up to. One wrong decision at this juncture and there would be no more kisses, no more Lex, and no more Gemma.

He peered over the top of the rock just as the chopper descended to the ground on top of the canyon rim.

Soon the engine noise died and the wop, wop ended. The helicopter had landed.

Gemma's forehead wrinkled. "I don't get it. They hovered over us and didn't see us. Then they landed above us on the canyon rim."

"There's a method to their madness. Before investors built the dam and started pumping water from Opal Springs, they cut a road into the side of the canyon. It's the only place you can drive down into this section of Crooked River."

"You mean the FBI thugs looked at the maps and figured out we would have come through here?"

"You're pretty smart. Not two hundred, but you're pretty and smart."

"And you've been spending too much time with little boys. Now, how are we going to get by them."

"We need to wait and see what they do. My guess is that, in about five minutes, a black van—"

"You mean that one?" Gemma pointed at the road cut into the opposite side of the canyon.

"Get your arm down." He pulled her behind the rock at the other end of the cove. "We need to do something about that white tank top. It's too visible."

"Well, I'm not taking it off."

"Keep your voice down, Gemma."

"You're acting like a little boy. Get your arm down. Keep your voice down. A bossy little boy."

"A bossy girl made me kiss her. By the way, do I kiss like a little boy, Gemma?"

"I don't—I mean I think—I don't have to answer that."

"Taking the fifth?"

"We shouldn't be discussing—you are crazy, Lex. These guys are getting out of the van. We need a plan to—"

"You would drive any guy crazy." He held Gemma's shoulders.

The look she gave him seemed to say, you are not just any guy, Lex James. But Lex was a complete newbie at interpreting those almond-shaped brown eyes. And sometimes he read what he wanted into other people's expressions. And at other times, he completely lost focus on the most important things.

"I know we need a plan to keep you safe, so you can testify and send those guys to prison where they belong. We'll wait and watch and plan based on who they leave here after dark. Trust me, they'll leave somebody."

For the next three hours they waited.

And for three hours, one plan replayed in his mind every time he looked at Gemma, a plan that brought her, the twins, and Lex together, permanently. But how could he be thinking this way about a woman he'd only known for a few hours?

Gemma's words answered that question. *You are crazy, Lex.*

Shortly after 8:00 p.m., all but one of the FBI agents got into the van. One of the men who climbed in was limping. The rattlesnake rim sniper.

The van slowly climbed the steep road out of the canyon and disappeared from sight.

Ten minutes later, the chopper took off.

At 9:00 p.m., darkness shrouded the deep canyon, though the sun was probably setting over the Cascades about now.

Gemma shifted her weight on the rock bench she sat on.

Her tank top glowed in the evening light like white clothes under a UV light.

"What are you staring at, Mr. James?"

"You. That tank top is glowing in the dark. When we make our move, I'll take off my brown T-shirt and you can slip it over—"

"Lex, your T-shirt absorbed a gallon of your sweat."

"But we swam in the river most of the way down here. It's relatively clean."

"I'm into *absolutely* clean. As in sterile. Besides, things that stink make me puke. I could get us killed if—"

"If you don't wear it, you will get us killed."

"Now that I think about it, we haven't eaten since breakfast. I don't have anything to puke."

"Gemma, what's gotten into you? You're nervous about this, aren't you?"

She leaned against him and nodded.

Lex circled her shoulders with his arms. "You know, things looked pretty bleak when the shooter was coming down the canyon rim after us. You prayed and we got a miracle."

"How can anyone call a rattlesnake a miracle?"

"Well, it was. And maybe you should try that again."

Gemma pressed her cheek against his chest and grew still.

Lex looked down at her and cupped her cheek.

Her ear lay over his heart. She was listening.

That Gemma would want to hear his heart beating, awakened something that hadn't been awake in—maybe it never had been, until now.

He had to keep this young woman alive. And the plan he was about to hatch would play an important role in accomplishing that goal. But the hardest part might be staying focused on the plan to keep them alive instead of the plan to keep Gemma.

She tilted her head up and peered into his eyes. "I'll pray, Lex. It's time, isn't it?"

"Yeah. Slip on my shirt and let's take a dip in the river. We need to be on the other side to get by them. But, while we're swimming, stay away from the dam. There's a strong current where the water goes through two twelve-foot tubes leading to the big turbines. If you get sucked in, those tubes will shoot you right into the blades and—"

"Stop it, Lex. If you're trying to freak me out, you did." She sat up and put her hands on his shoulders. "Will you swim downstream of me? Keep me away from the dam? Please?"

"You got it."

Five minutes later they crawled out of the river on the east bank, well above the dam.

Lex raised his head. He peeked over the bank and scanned the dirt roadway beyond the dam.

68

No one.

"The buildings are a quarter-mile down this road. That's also where the road coming down from the top comes in. We'll need to take it slow and easy through that part."

Lex led Gemma down the left side of the road lined with small trees and bushes that grew along the river's edge.

The road turned to the left as they approached the lights around the buildings. Before those lights could expose them, Lex stepped off the road and made his way through the bushes beside it.

Gemma hooked her fingers around his belt and followed close behind in the darkness.

The bushes ended.

Lex stopped, while he sought a way to cross the open area.

Someone's cell phone rang.

Lex waited.

A man's voice spoke softly.

Lex couldn't hear the words above the sound of the river.

The voice grew louder. The man came into view, walking their way, talking on his phone.

From the few words Lex could distinguish, this guy sounded like one of the FBI agents.

A second man, wearing a uniform, followed a few steps behind.

Probably a security guard.

The light from the building might reveal Gemma and Lex. He dropped into the darkness behind a bush and listened.

Gemma knelt behind him.

"So you want me to stay here all night. But what about the chopper?"

"That's the FBI agent," he whispered to Gemma.

The man pulled the phone from his ear and swore at the device in his hand.

"Did you lose the connection?" the second man came alongside.

"Yeah."

"The reception is not so good down here in the canyon. But, if you walk a couple of hundred yards up the hill on the canyon road, it's much better."

"Thanks. I'll try that." The FBI agent turned and took the road that climbed out of the canyon.

This was the opportunity Lex had hoped for. One man to elude or overpower, a man not bent on killing them, the security guard. But would he try to alert the FBI agent? Lex needed to prevent that, somehow.

"Wait here, Gemma. When I toss a rock back here, come immediately as long as Mr. FBI hasn't returned."

"Be careful, Lex. I'm praying for you."

He touched her cheek and stepped out of the bushes.

The security guard had turned and walked away from Lex's position, back toward the buildings on this side of the river. The man stopped near the small bridge.

Hopefully, he would take the bridge to check the facilities on the other side of the river. That would give them an opportunity to slip by.

Lex turned and scanned the road where the FBI thug had gone.

No signs of him, yet. But with only the light of stars, bright as they were under Central Oregon skies, Lex could see less than a hundred yards.

He turned back to the security guard who had been clearly visible in the light around the buildings.

The guard had vanished.

Not good.

Lex crept out into the road far enough to circle the tree near the entrance to the bridge.

The guard wasn't on the road and he wasn't on the bridge.

A telltale tingling ran up the back of Lex's neck.

"Hands on your head and don't move."

The guard must've played ring-around-the-tree and gotten behind Lex.

He placed his hands on his head and turned slowly toward the guard.

"I said don't move."

Lex stopped moving.

What kind of story had the agent told this guy? Lex sought words that would answer his question. "Sir, do you know who I am?"

"You are the guy who killed a U.S. Marshal and the young woman, your accomplice, is here somewhere too."

More lies from the FBI. "No, sir. The rogue FBI agent is the one who killed the marshal. I'm Lex James."

"What?"

"Please keep your voice down, sir. That FBI agent might decide to kill us all."

"But there was a whole team of FBI agents looking for you—uh, for the killer and the woman. They even had a chopper?"

"I take it you've heard of me, sir. I investigate government corruption and report on it in The American Motto. This is one of the worst cases I've come across. If this *team* as you call them, kills Gemma and me, they'll get off scot free and the whole nation will suffer."

Silence.

Lex waited. The guard probably knew Lex's reputation, but did this man believe him?

"You got any ID?"

"Yes."

"Step over behind the tree and you can show it to me."

Lex hesitated. He couldn't risk being spotted by the agent.

"Go ahead. No one on the road can see us there."

While it was reassuring that the guard considered what Lex had told him, this still called for caution. But they needed to hurry before the phone call up the hill ended.

Lex slowly pulled his soggy wallet from his cargo shorts. He opened it, flipped out his driver's license and handed the wallet to the guard. "You'll see a laminated business card on the flip side of my driver's license."

"Well I'll be—suppose you tell me again why the FBI is after you."

"Sir, this isn't any ordinary FBI operation. These men were sent here by some corrupt people in high places in the DOJ. This is a black operation to kill a witness who can bring down all the players in this conspiracy. I'm trying to keep her alive, and so I'm a target too. If they even suspect that you were helping me, they'll kill you."

The security guard, a man who looked about retirement age, stroked his short beard several times. "Where's the witness?"

"I'm right here." Gemma crept around the tree from behind them with a big rock in her hand.

"And you were going to brain me with that rock?"

"I was going to try."

"Gemma, you don't follow directions very well."

She dropped the rock and hurried to Lex's side.

The security guard shook his head. "I thought something wasn't right about those guys. Especially that one they call Blade. Gave me the creeps. Okay. You two can go. I'll think of some story to cover you."

"Thanks," Gemma said. "Have you got any drinking water around here?"

"Follow me. We'll go through the building and you can grab a bottle on the way."

A minute later, Lex and Gemma crept into the bushes along the river a few yards above the spring. Each had a bottle of water in hand.

Once they slipped behind the bushes, they opened their bottles and drank.

Correction, Gemma guzzled.

"Whoa. You're going to get sick, Gemma."

"First you said drinking bad water would make me puke. Now you're saying good water will make me puke. You enjoy torturing me don't you, Mr. James?"

Voices came from near the buildings seventy-five yards up the river.

"Hush, Gemma."

The voices grew louder.

One grew angry. "If you saw them, where did they go?"

"Didn't you see them?"

"No. Are you forgetting to tell me something, old man?"

"Here's what I think. They ran down the road toward the dam but must've cut straight up the hill and got on the road you were on ... somewhere above you."

"Here's what I think, old man ... you let them get away. And, if you lied to an FBI agent, that's a crime. You will die of old age in the federal penitentiary."

"If that's the way you guys work—intimidating good American citizens—somebody needs to clean house in the DOJ."

"You talk like that and you might not make it to retirement."

The voices grew quieter.

Lex had heard enough.

Gemma put her mouth near his ear. "We've got to stop these guys, or they can do things like that to any American. We'll lose our country."

"Right now, we just need to get out of here."

With their thirst mostly quenched, Lex led Gemma downstream toward the finger of Lake Billy Chinook that poked into the Crooked River canyon.

The moon hadn't risen yet, and they had no trail to follow on this isolated stretch of Crooked River.

In the darkness, the tangle of bushes snagged their clothing and scratched their bare arms and legs.

Gemma didn't complain, even when the canyon walls forced them to ford the river to get on the other side.

They crossed in shallow rapids, but the knee-deep water nearly swept them away.

After they stepped from the water onto the rocky river bank, a muffled rattling sound came from a bush on Gemma's left.

Lex hooked her waist and lifted her, then he set her down on his right side.

But the buzzing grew louder.

Gemma drew a sharp breath and froze.

Lex scooped her up and carried her farther away from the rattlesnake's warning buzz.

"It's okay, Gemma. He was just warning us to keep out of his hunting grounds."

Her grip around his neck didn't loosen. If anything, it tightened, nearly choking him.

"If you'll loosen that chokehold, I'll set you down."

"Are we safe?" Her words came wrapped in a hoarse whisper.

"We're safe."

Gemma's fear of snakes seemed to be a phobia, irrational. Evil people could shoot at them, and she didn't panic. But one little rattler, even one that gave them fair warning, paralyzed her.

The complexity of Gemma Saint baffled him, but that only prodded Lex to learn more about this young woman who seemed to be claiming huge chunks of his heart. If she were to ask for it right now, Lex James was inclined to give it to her.

You are a fool, Lex James.

Lex took the vermin's voice in his mind and pictured feeding it to that rattlesnake.

He could protect Gemma from the reptilian version, but human rattlesnakes sent by someone in the DOJ were another species and another matter. To keep Gemma safe, he needed to take her to a spot near the lake before morning.

They moved forward again. And, in the darkness filled with obstacles, progress became painfully slow. But Lex's plan for tomorrow did not require them to make their escape until mid-morning or later. They should be able to get some much-needed rest.

Gemma touched his bare shoulder. "You can have your shirt back. It might smell like me now, but I wouldn't want you to get all scratched up by these bushes."

Smell like Gemma? He would keep that shirt forever, if reminded him of her. These growing feelings seemed to be more than just the comradery of shared danger. Like her name, Gemma Saint was—

"Well, if you don't want it ..."

"Sorry, Gemma. I'm running on fumes. I'll take my shirt. Would you like to stop for a nap? We'll need to be rested for what's coming tomorrow."

"Wasn't going to say anything, but I've dozed off on my feet a couple of times. This is my second night in a row without sleep."

She hadn't asked about what was coming tomorrow. Maybe Gemma was too tired to think about it. Another sign that he needed to find a place for them to rest.

After passing on two scrubby trees, Lex found a tree with enough foliage to hide them from anyone in a helicopter and with enough room for two tired bodies.

The ground was soft and, under the tree, covered with a bed of dead leaves.

He and Gemma gathered tree boughs, bunch grass, anything soft that they could find, and piled it all against the trunk of the tree to make pillows.

Lex stretched out on his side of the trunk and rolled onto his side.

Gemma built her bed on the other side of the tree. Probably to maintain some semblance of propriety.

Fatigue so deep that his muscles quivered threatened to put Lex quickly under its anesthesia. He tried to relax and simply succumb. He didn't need to try very hard.

"Lex?" Gemma's voice.

He had his shirt back. What was it now. "Yeah."

"I've heard people say that rattlesnakes slither into people's sleeping bags to get warm. They wake up in the morning and—"

"Gemma, people say a lot of things."

"You know that I don't like snakes. Could we wake up with snakes beside us?"

"Any warm-blooded animal bigger than the snake is a danger, an enemy. The snake will either slither away to escape, or bite if it has to defend itself."

"What if the snakes *like* me? I could wake up with snakes on both sides of me."

"I don't get it, Gemma. People shoot at us and chase us and you're cool as a cucumber. But one thought of going under water or of snakes and you—"

"I can't help it. Those thoughts make me antsy. They give me diarrhea of the mouth."

"That is a mixed-up metaphor."

"It's what my mother calls it when I get this way."

"I thought you were sleepy."

"I will be." Gemma stood and moved her makeshift pillow to his side of the tree. She stretched out on the ground beside him and laid her head on her pillow.

She scooted closer until she bumped into his knees. "At least the snakes can't get on both sides of me. Please ..." her voice grew soft. "... don't tell my accountability group at church. If you do, I'll never, ever ... hear the end of ... the ... end ..." Gemma's soft, regular breathing started.

It soothed Lex. Her breathing signified that they had survived the day, a day when several of the nation's best, or worst, had tried to kill them and failed.

He curled an arm around Gemma and soon drifted into his own place of peace.

Lex's eyes popped open.

The sun was up. Way up. He glanced at his watch. 10:00 a.m.

Gemma lay facing him now, breathing softly. Despite their ordeal yesterday that had physically ravaged their bodies and taxed their minds, Gemma appeared unmarred by any of it. She was peacefully resting, absolutely and beautifully perfect.

For Lex James she seemed perfect. And his two boys appeared to have rapidly jumped to that same conclusion. And with their two hundred, how could they be wrong?

The droning sound of an engine replaced his thoughts of Gemma.

The sound grew louder.

Lex rose to his knees and turned toward the noise.

Please let it be a boat.

He peered through the tree branches that hung around them and looked toward the mouth of the Crooked River. It lay only seventy-five yards to the north. And beyond that, Lake Billy Chinook.

Their nighttime trek had ended right where they needed to be. Maybe it was a sign of how their day would go.

From somewhere behind Lex, came the telltale sounds of a helicopter.

Or was that a sign of how their day would go?

Gemma jumped at the sound of the chopper and rose to her knees beside him. "What's happening?"

"It's good news and bad news."

"After yesterday, can I have the good news first?" She opened her water bottle and drained the last few ounces from it.

He pointed toward the Lake. "See that boat pulling in?"

She nodded.

"This is a popular picnicking and fishing spot, but there's only room for one boat."

A boy about twelve years old sat on the bow with a rope in hand as the big boat nosed in to the shore.

"That could be our ticket out of here?"

Gemma pointed downstream. "Can't we walk out of here? There's a bridge down there, somewhere. I drove over it once, when I went to Culver."

"The chopper just landed on the rim above Opal Springs."

"The Fibbies."

"What did you call them, Gemma?"

"They're not really FBI, not good cops. So I think we should call them Fibbies. It's what comes out when you try to pronounce the acronym."

"Then Fibbies they are. Looks like we'll have to wait a bit for our ride out of here. By then, we'll know if the Fibbies are doing what I think they're gonna do."

"You mean the bad news?"

"Yeah. They'll figure out that we passed them during the night, and they'll sweep the canyon all the way to the lake. We can't be here when they finish their sweep."

"Wouldn't they just fly over in their helicopter?"

"That didn't work yesterday. And that tree we slept under—they couldn't have spotted us from the air. No, they'll be on foot."

"So what are we going to do, steal that nice family's boat?"

"No. We'll borrow it."

"That's not how they'll see it."

"Gemma, after it's all over, we'll return the boat and they'll be understanding of our patriotic intentions."

"Sure they will."

The boat had tied up to shore. A woman and four kids climbed off it, while a forty-something man handed them boxes, packs, and camping chairs.

"Looks like an all-day picnic. But we can't be here when the trigger-happy Fibbies show up. We might endanger an innocent family."

"So we steal their boat to keep them safe?"

"Gemma, you have the doggonedest way of putting things."

"Lead the way, Lex. I want to see how you do this."

"Wait. Let's listen for a moment."

In the distance, occasional cracking sounds came from upstream.

"They're coming down the canyon like hunters on a deer drive."

"On a what?"

"Never mind. They're less than a mile upstream. We've got about fifteen minutes to turn that boat into our pirate ship."

"And then the Fibbies really will be chasing a couple of criminals."

"Like I said, you have the doggonedest way of putting things."

"And they will have the doggonedest way of putting us in prison."

"No, Gemma. The only things they want to put ... are bullets in us."

Chapter 12

Blade stood beside the chopper on the Canyon rim above Opal Springs evaluating his options for spinning their latest failure. Carr would call any minute for his morning report and all Blade had to offer was plan B.

Whenever plan A fails, it's because someone didn't know something they needed to know, or because someone was incompetent. Bladen Sikes was not incompetent. But Kirby and Walker were.

Kirby got himself snake bitten when he had Saint and James pinned down. And Walker let them slip past him last night, though the night watchman may have been complicit.

An old swamp rock tune played on Sikes's phone. He chuckled. Carr's song. Something about who'll stop the rain. Whoever that was, it surely wasn't Carr.

"Sikes."

"Carr here. I didn't get *the call*, so I assume you still haven't gotten them."

"My two young guys, Kirby and Walker, let us down."

"You chose your team, Sikes."

"I did. Within some pretty heavy ideological restrictions, if you'll recall. Look, Kirby let himself get bitten by a rattlesnake when he had them in his sights. Walker let them slip past him last night."

No reply.

Carr was probably red-faced and smoking from his ears about now.

"We might get them in the next few minutes. But if we don't, I recommend we go with plan B ... in parallel with what we're doing."

"I don't know if I should trust you to go any further, Sikes. You screw up and we all could go down. Now, remind me what plan B entails."

"We keep looking for them using the chopper, but we also nab James's boys. He'll play ball to save his kids."

"Isn't KC Daniels watching them? You hurt her and you'll have half this nation, the military, and all of law enforcement nailing you on the wall and tanning your sorry hide."

"We won't touch a hair on her head."

"How will Lex James hear about your, uh ... bait?"

"If he slips away from us this morning, he'll check on his boys. If he doesn't get away, then we have nothing to worry about."

"So, the scope of the mission keeps creeping." Carr muttered something indistinguishable, then swore at Blade, at his men, and at Gemma Saint.

"Speaking of Ms. Saint, the Intel you gave us was bogus. She's not some sweet, naïve little college girl. She's as tough as nails, can run like the wind, and is all heart. If she wasn't, Lex James couldn't have kept her or himself alive yesterday."

Carr sighed into the phone. "Okay. We go with plan B."

"We're on it."

Carr ended the call.

Blade drew a deep breath and exhaled slowly.

He was seldom thankful for anything that happened in life, but he was thankful for Carr's agreement on plan B because, while Walker watched Opal Springs last night, Blade and Kirby had taken the two kids.

Chapter 13

"It's now or never, Gemma."

Lex was actually going to commit grand theft. Soon Gemma would be a pirate on Lake Billy Chinook sailing—rather motoring—on some nice family's stolen Bayliner.

Lex hooked her arm and pulled. "Come on. It took us five minutes to sneak over here. The Fibbies could be here in less than ten minutes, Gemma."

She scanned the shoreline of the lake up to the family's picnic area near the mouth of the river. With the boat between them and the picnickers, she and Lex could climb onboard, untie the boat, and be ready to go—No! No! No! This was crazy.

"Lex, how do we know the keys will be there? Do you know how to drive this thing?"

"You worry too much. This is an isolated area. They'll leave the keys. And, yes, I've piloted boats on this lake. My friend has one. I've driven his."

Lex took a step toward the twenty-five-foot boat which rocked gently in the ripples at the confluence of the river and the lake.

She jerked Lex to a stop. "What kind of boat did your friend have, a dinghy with a motor?"

"Do I detect a lack of confidence? No. It was bigger than a dinghy."

"How much bigger?"

"Have I let you down, Gemma? Forget it. We don't have time for this." Lex scooped her up and set her on the bow of the boat. "Slide in. I'm right behind you."

Gemma climbed in and crouched in the boat, trying to keep her head down so she couldn't be seen. "I've been kidnapped by a pirate."

Lex scurried to the wheel. "Keys are here. *Bon voyage.*" He hit the starter and the motor turned.

With the twist of a key and the push of a button, Gemma Saint had become a felon, a modern-day pirate. "Lex, when do we hoist the jolly roger?"

"Daddy, he's taking our boat!" An eight- or nine-year-old girl on the shore pointed at them.

"I think they hoisted it for us." Lex waved at them. "Sorry, folks. It's an emergency. We're borrowing it, but we'll bring it back."

The engine revved.

Lex cranked the wheel toward the lake.

The boat leaned toward the port side like a banking airplane and zoomed away from shore into the lake.

Gemma looked back at the family on the shore.

The man stood in firing position, holding a handgun.

"Lex, he's going to shoot!" Gemma flattened herself on the deck.

Lex left one hand on the wheel but ducked out of the shooter's sight.

A loud pop sounded.

Lex raised his head enough to look back at the picnic spot. "It's okay, Gemma. He's shooting over our heads. Probably doesn't want to damage his boat."

"That's a man's priorities for you."

"Would you rather he demonstrated a woman's priorities?"

Gemma rose to her knees and risked looking at the shooter.

Two men armed with assault rifles emerged from the trees by the mouth of the river and looked their way.

"Lex... it's the Fibbies and they saw us."

"Doesn't make much difference."

"What do you mean?" She hooked his arm and tried to turn him around to face her.

"Stop it, Gemma. I'm driving."

"Driving under the influence."

He twisted away from her and put both hands on the wheel. "Influence of what?"

"Insanity."

"Think about it, Gemma. The Fibbies were going to show up regardless. And, as soon as they talked to that family, they would know it was us who took the boat."

Lex cranked the throttle open until the Bayliner planed on the calm Lake.

Gemma strained to make out what was happening back at the picnic area. Her peripheral vision caught a small black object on the seat beside her.

Binoculars.

She grabbed them, adjusted the zoom, and focused on the family and the armed men. "Lex, one of the Fibbies has a cell phone in his ear."

"How can you see that far?" He turned toward Gemma. "Oh. Binoculars. But them calling—that's not good."

"You've got that right. He's probably calling for that helicopter. Lex, where can we hide this thing?"

Lex glanced her way. "You mean the boat? There's always Davy Jones' Locker."

"We can't sink that nice family's boat."

"You keep calling them nice. Gemma, they shot at us."

"They only shot to warn us. You can't hold that against them. But what are we supposed to do now? Go down with the ship? You know that me and water don't exactly—"

"Quiet for a minute. I'm thinking."

"You should have been thinking before we stole the boat. Now the Fibbies really *are* after two criminals. Lex James, Peter Pan one moment, Captain Hook the next."

"Gemma, I need to concentrate."

She would let him concentrate alright, while she concentrated on his rear end, where she would like to plant her shoe.

"Eureka! I've got it!" Lex pointed a finger at something ahead of them on the shore.

"This isn't a bathtub, Lex. It's a lake."

"I think we can get there in less than ten minutes."

"Seriously, Archimedes? A bathtub in ten minutes?"

He ignored her and opened the throttle all the way. The powerful engine roared. The Bayliner accelerated until the water sizzled under its hull.

In the strong wind, Gemma's hair lashed her face like a whip. She moved forward beside Lex, to the protection of the windshield. "In ten minutes, their helicopter could be hovering over us. They will shoot this nice family's boat full of holes ... and us too."

Lex looked her way and a smirk tweaked one side of his mouth. "Only if we're on it. But maybe we can save the boat and ourselves."

This guy was clearly delusional. Gemma didn't reply. You don't argue with a madman. Somebody famous said that ... G. K. Chester something or other.

Lex pulled one hand from the wheel. "There's only one catch to this."

Maybe there were some exceptions to that arguing-with-a-madman rule. And Gemma would take exception to any escape via water, unless they were in the boat. "Lex, you're not getting me into that Lake. It's cold and it's deep."

"Exactly—there it is." Lex pointed to their right, to some spot on the shore.

"There is what?"

He was pointing to the land, not water.

But his "one catch" worried her.

Lex cut the speed to less than half of what it had been. "Find me something to tie to the wheel. You know, to hold it straight."

Three life jackets with Velcro straps lay on a seat behind Gemma. She grabbed all three and handed one to Lex.

He stooped and looked under the wheel. "Great. This should work."

The familiar, dreaded wopping sound came from somewhere in the distance. Gemma scanned the sky until she spotted it.

A mile or two ahead and to their left, a lone chopper turned a semicircle until it was headed toward them.

Gemma grabbed the binoculars and focused on the helicopter.

"It's them, Lex." She pointed to the familiar looking chopper that couldn't be more than a minute or two away.

Lex steered closer to shore then grabbed all three life preservers and velcro'd them onto the wheel. When he finished, he took off his T-shirt and stretched it over the topmost life preserver creating a crude human torso.

A baseball cap lay in a cubbyhole beside the wheel. He placed it on top of a life preserver.

The dummy at the wheel had been replaced by another dummy, one that *might* look real from a hundred yards away.

But this left only one place for her and Lex, Lake Billy Chinook.

Lex grabbed her hand. "I need you to take a deep breath and then start counting to a hundred. Count slowly."

"What else? Stop breathing? Drown?"

"I'll do all the rest."

"So you're going to panic and drown for me?"

She looked at the shore thirty yards away. Gemma would drown or die of claustrophobic fear before they could swim underwater to shore. And, if they didn't slip into the water on the starboard side, the Fibbies might see them abandon ship. Then they would be shot.

Either way Gemma Saint was about to die. When that happened, getting shot had her vote.

Lex took both of her hands, lifted her over the side, and lowered her into the chilly water.

She gasped when it reached her waist. Maybe she was about to get the worst of both deaths. Claustrophobia, then a bullet through her head.

Lex leaped over the side. On the way down he said, "Take a deep breath."

Her breathing had turned to panting, partly from the cold, but mostly from thoughts about what was coming.

Gemma tried to draw a deep breath. She had most of it sucked in when Lex hit the water, feet first, like an arrow.

Lex still held her hand in his strong grasp. He yanked her under water with him, and he went deep.

The boat above them continued on its merry way, guided by the dummy that was oblivious to whatever was coming.

Count, Gemma, like Lex said.

One ... two ... three ... four, five, six, seven, eight— Now, the numbers flew through her mind as if they came from an auctioneer's mouth. Somewhere past fifty, something told her it was time to breathe.

Lex towed her through the water with one hand, while his legs kicked like a frog. He pawed at the water with his other hand.

Gemma looked up at the water surface several feet above them. She needed to surface, now. The cold water stung her eyes. The pressure hurt her ears. But, more importantly, she had to breathe, *now*, or she was going to lose it.

She tried to break free from Lex's grip.

That got-to-breathe feeling drove the last vestiges of her sanity away. She opened her mouth to scream.

Water came in.

She blew it out, trying to clear her mouth, but only choked.

Dizziness and a buzzing in her head intensified.

So this is what drowning is like.

No! She couldn't drown.

But how could she not drown?

Gemma screamed, and bubbles escaped her mouth as the last bit of air left her lungs. Empty now, her chest crumpled under the water pressure like a deflating vacuum-sealed bag. And the only thing she could fill it with was water.

Still Lex pulled her toward something dark that appeared a short distance ahead.

Lightning flashed. A thunderclap hit her head. It pounded her ears with a painful impact.

Dazed and choking on the water, she'd inhaled, Gemma's strength faded from her legs and arms.

Then she broke the surface of the water in a strange, dark place.

Her feet touched bottom.

Lex held her by both shoulders. "Gemma?"

She coughed and splattered him in the face with a geyser of water, water that had been blocking her airway.

Air. She was breathing it. She hadn't drowned.

"Are you okay, Gemma."

"Maybe. Just... let me... catch my breath."

"While you're doing that, I think you should turn around, put your eyes at water level, and look out the mouth of this cave."

Gemma tried to comply, but still wasn't quite in tune with reality. When she did look, her body stiffened.

A hundred yards away, the nice family's boat floated. Two-hundred yards away more pieces of the Bayliner floated. Flames and smoke came from most of the debris in the lake.

As far up as the roof of the cave allowed her to see, a pillar of black smoke rose into the azure sky.

She looked at Lex. "We destroyed that poor family's boat."

"Gemma, the Fibbies nuked it with an RPG. Maybe one of those thermobaric ones that works like a Hellfire Missile."

"What if they drop one on us?"

"They don't drop them. They shoot them. But you can hardly see this cave when the lake is this high. It's just a narrow slit at water level. They have no clue that it opens up inside. Only the locals know about the cave. Come on. In the back we can sit on rocks out of the water."

"What if they land close by and come looking for us?"

"Think about it for a minute, Gemma."

It didn't take a minute, now that she had regained most of her faculties. "The Fibbies just blew up somebody's boat. The government attacked civilians and they used military weapons to do it. They have to leave, don't they? "

"You got your two-hundred back, didn't you?"

She glared at him but didn't reply.

"You were right," Lex said. "They can't let themselves be associated with this. And, this time of year, there are enough people on the lake that there'll be witnesses. This is the end of them using that helicopter. But other people will come, lookie-loos and then the Sheriff."

"So what do we do?"

"We have two options. Both are risky."

"Lex James, if you think hooking up with me to get your story was risky, hooking up with you—you're downright dangerous."

"Hooking up—that's an interesting way to put it." He paused.

She looked his way and saw his mischievous grin.

"But, Gemma, would you rather I *hadn't* helped you?"

She replayed her non-stop thriller that began shortly after meeting Lex.

Then Gemma looked at the burning pieces of boat strewn across the Lake.

She didn't reply.

Chapter 14

Blade's secure phone displayed 11:55 a.m. when it played the chopper song. Drake's tune. He must have eliminated Saint and James.

"Saint James." The pun did seem to fit those two. Blade chuckled, then answered the call. "Sikes."

"Enola Gay returning home. Mission accomplished." Drake's voice, cheerful and confidant.

"How did this little drama play out, Drake?"

"We caught the boat about halfway up Billy Chinook. I brought us in fast and Petrelli scored a direct hit with a thermobaric grenade."

"You actually used the SMAW?"

"Blade, you wanted them dead, right?"

"Yes. And you're sure they are?"

"They were both on the Bayliner when the grenade hit. After the fireball and smoke cleared, about two-hundred pieces of boat floated in the lake, most of it still burning. After we saw that, we made a quick getaway, took the chopper home, and disappeared before anyone could figure out what happened. Now, are you satisfied?"

"So you're at the cabin?"

"Yes. We're at the cabin, as planned, awaiting further orders, *sir*." Drakes tone had turned disrespectful on the last word.

Blade made a mental note of that in case questions arose about the chopper team's loyalties. "Stay there. I'll call if we need you. We have one other matter to attend to, then we can all go home and wait for our reward after the election."

"Carr will come through for us, won't he?" Drake asked.

"Of course. By then he'll be director. Why do you ask?"

"This has been a lot more work than it should have been. We've taken too many risks. I just wanted to be sure your buddy, Max, fully appreciates what we've done for him."

"Max Carr appreciates it, Drake. After the new president is sworn in, we'll all get our cushy assignments and promotions. But, for now, just lay low until you hear from me."

Blade ended the call.

He was tempted to conclude that Gemma Saint had gone the way of all good saints ... martyrdom. But she had slipped through their fingers twice. Two miraculous escapes.

The last thing Blade needed was a third one.

Chapter 15

University of Colorado Hospital, Aurora, Colorado
"He's waking up."

Marshal Cody Cottrell opened his eyes. He quickly regretted it when the piercing light stabbed his pupils. Cody slammed his eyelids down. That reaction sent pulses of pain reverberating through his head.

He needed to see the source of the voices and to see where he was.

Cody drew a hand to his forehead to shield his eyes and tried again.

"Mr. Cottrell?" A man in what looked like scrubs hovered over him and studied his face.

"I'm Marshal Cottrell."

"That's right, Marshal Cottrell. And that's a very good sign."

"Why? Do you need a U.S. marshal for protection or—"

Protection? Gemma! She's in danger!

"I need to get out of here. It's important."

"All in good time. I'm Dr. John. You were shot in the head. Somehow the bullet glanced off your skull without penetrating it. You are one fortunate marshal. But we need to keep you here until we see the full extent of your injury and to help in your recovery."

The pain in Cody's head seemed like a sound, a tone that brought pain with it and made concentrating nearly impossible. He pushed through the pain to speak again. "How long have I been here?"

"You were shot about thirty-six hours ago and we've had you here at University Hospital for a little over twenty-four hours."

"A day and a half?" Cody prayed that Gemma had gotten away and was able to hide. But, even if she had, she would need his help or, the odds were, she would be killed. "Have any other marshal's been here?"

"As a matter of fact, one of your colleagues is outside your room as we speak. You can have a couple of minutes to exchange any important information, then we need to keep it quiet in your room. We may give you something to help you sleep while your brain recovers. Would you like me to send him in?"

"Who is it?"

"I believe it's Marshal Shaw."

Shaw? Alarms sounded in Cody's muddled mind, bringing more pain and something else. Shaw was on Cody's list of potential leakers, a list he'd constructed to determine who leaked Gemma Saint's WITSEC identity information. If it was Shaw, maybe he would slip up while talking with Cody, ask the wrong question or something. It was worth a try.

"Yes, please send in Marshal Shaw."

Cody closed his eyes and tried to collect as much mental composure as that tormenting tone in his head would allow.

A shadow dimmed the lights penetrating Cody's eyelids. He opened his eyes only enough to see Shaw's face.

"Hey, Cottrell. You gave us a real scare, man. How are you feeling?"

"Never had a headache like this in my life."

"Beats the alternative, doesn't it?"

"That depends on where you're going next, Shaw. You made any arrangements for that?"

Shaw was a vocal skeptic about all things religious and other worldly. Goading him before addressing the issue at hand couldn't hurt. It would irritate him, maybe enough to make him slip up.

"Don't need any arrangements, dude. It's just the big sleep. But I do need to know what you know about who shot you? Did you see anything or hear anything? Right now, we have next to nothing to go on."

Cody had nothing to offer. But saying that wouldn't help him evaluate Shaw. Maybe it was time for some subtext with a little pretext. "I heard something before the shot. And I heard the shot. It sounded like a—I don't know. My head hurts every time I try to think."

"Are you sure you can't tell me what you heard. And the gunshot, what kind of handgun was it?"

Cody hadn't said it was a handgun. "Did you find the bullet? The doc said it bounced off my head."

"Off your head and out a window. We couldn't find it."

Cody grimaced as he prepared for the pain but met Shaw's gaze with as much scrutiny as Cody could muster. "I'd say it was a Glock."

A Glock was good choice for the gun he hadn't heard. It was the standard issue for the FBI. They'd just inked an eighty-five-million-dollar contract with Glock.

Had Shaw flinched? Many people owned Glocks, but ...

Maybe Cody could drop another threatening clue to Shaw.

Cody's head pain crescendoed in a pulse that nearly knocked him out. Maybe dropping more leading clues could get a defenseless Cody killed. "Shaw, I think this headache has muddled my brain. Can't think right now. I wouldn't put much stock in anything I told you ... whatever it was. I can't even remember now."

"Get some rest. Maybe we'll find that bullet and solve the mystery."

"Before you go ... who's covering for me, for ... you know?"

"That would be me. Get some rest, dude. Talk to you later."

If Shaw was covering for Cody, that meant Shaw would know about Gemma. Well, he would know about her before she ran. With the FBI at the U.S. Marshal's disposal, they would find Gemma before long.

He couldn't let that happen. Headache or not, concussion or trauma to Cody's brain—none of that mattered. The marshals had never lost anyone who had followed the rules of WITSEC and Cody's charge, Gemma Saint, was not going to be the first.

Not even if I have to sneak out of this place to find her. And not even if it kills me.

Chapter 16

"Gemma, we've got to get out of here." Lex studied her face for a moment in the semi-darkness of the cave.

Long, dark hair hanging in damp curls. Large, almond-shaped brown eyes questioning him. Even wearing her serious look instead of her smile, she was absolutely, spectacularly—"

"Lex? Are you even listening to me?"

He was now. "Yeah."

"The Sheriff's boat is out there."

"You mean the one with the big Yamaha outboard on it?"

"Of course. It says Sheriff on the side, as plain as day. Lex, where is your mind right now?"

He tried to wipe the silly grin from his face.

"Never mind. Don't answer that." Gemma paused. "There are two Jet Skis and some people swimming in the water. So how are we going to get away? If anyone sees us, we'll have too many questions to answer. If they took us in for questioning, or anything like that, we could be spotted by the Fibbies, maybe even be on local TV. We wouldn't make it through the day alive."

"What an optimist. You're just a little ray of sunshine."

"I could be if you can tell me how we're going to get out of here."

"I'm going to slip out and take a look at the cliff above us and the shoreline from here to Round Butte Dam at the north end of the lake. Those are our two options, other than getting picked up by the sheriff."

"Please, Lex, don't let anyone see you. If you do, we're dead. Those guys won't let us get away again. They would take whatever extreme measures they needed to—"

"Extreme measures? Gemma, they shot an RPG at us and blew our boat to smithereens. I don't know how much more extreme you can get."

She leaned her head against his shoulder. "I don't want to find out. Be careful out there, because I ..."

He waited.

She left her head leaning against his shoulder and didn't seem to want to move.

How would she feel once the danger was gone? Could Lex James be so fortunate as to have Gemma in his life, permanently? Not if he couldn't keep her alive, and that began with getting out of this cave undetected.

Lex cupped her cheek. "I'll be careful."

Gemma sat up and sighed.

Lex drew a sharp breath as he slid down into the chilling water.

* * *

How long had Lex been gone? Fifteen, twenty minutes?

Gemma hadn't anticipated it would take that long to check the cliff. Maybe the holdup was trying to remain hidden from the people investigating the boat.

If they caught Lex, she would be on her own, completely and totally alone. That idea was no more appealing than swimming thirty yards under water.

Out on the lake, two or three engines started. In a few seconds, the noise faded into the background. We're the police leaving?

Splashes sounded near the cave opening.

Was it Lex?

She slid to the water's edge, sat on a rock, and dangled her feet in the water. Gemma leaned down, peering out of the cave to see if all the boats and Jet Skis were gone.

Something grabbed her foot and tugged. She gasped and yanked her foot free.

Lex popped up out of the water.

She put a hand on the top of his head and shoved him back under. He deserved it. This was not a time for pranks.

Lex surfaced a few feet away and climbed out of the water. "Did the Loch Ness Monster come after you, Gemma?"

She shook her head. "Little boys never grow up, do they?"

"It's the curse of the Lost Boys. But Captain Hook just left in his ship. If we go now, we're home free."

Gemma stood up on the rock where she'd been sitting. "They all left?"

"Yep. Boats and Jet Skis all gone, at least for now."

"What about the cliff?"

"It's still there."

"Lex James, what did you find? Are we about to climb Mount Everest?"

He climbed out of the water and stood on the rock beside her. "Not Everest. More like Mount Gotcha."

"What's that supposed to mean? We get to fall and do the Fibbies job for them?"

"Not exactly."

"Lex, since the sheriff's boat left, can't we just walk and swim along the shore to the dam? There's a road there."

"If we work our way carefully up the cliff, following the grass, we can get two-thirds of the way up with no real climbing. But ..."

"Then comes the gotcha?"

"I can't see the top that well from down here. The last one-hundred feet is a vertical cliff that has tumbled down in places. The problem is, if the grass stops, we have to climb rocks. And the only places we can climb are where the cliff has collapsed. Wherever the cliff collapses ..."

"Rock slides? That's what you're afraid of, isn't it?"

He nodded.

Gemma closed the distance between them and circled his shoulders with her arms. "If we were to die leaving here, I don't want my legacy to be that I died doing something really stupid. Let's take the shoreline to the dam. Please, Lex."

"Even if it might require a little underwater swimming?"

"I survived that already. How far is this trek to the dam?"

"Half a mile. Maybe three quarters. Probably a couple of hundred yards in the water. Hopefully, none under it."

She released her hold on Lex, took his hand and pulled him with her into the water. Even when the water level reached her chin, Gemma remained calm. How had she managed that?

Pirate ships. Lost boys. She'd experienced it all today. And Lex had gotten her through it. After all, Peter Pan did teach Wendy to fly. She even sang a song about that.

Sometimes Lex made her feel like she could fly, but Gemma wasn't going to burst into song no matter what Lex taught her.

* * *

"At least they didn't arrest us." Gemma's big brown eyes looked up at him, oozing innocence.

"How could any red-blooded man arrest you after that performance?"

"Performance? Lex, we didn't do anything wrong. We walked along the shoreline because we had no choice. And we weren't going to blow up the dam. We were trapped by circumstances beyond our control. That's the only reason we walked into that restricted area."

"Gemma Saint turns on the charm and the hearts of men melt. They stumble over themselves to do her bidding. They—"

"That's enough, Lex! My charm doesn't seem to have any effect on the Fibbies. Let's just hope this ride to Madras the security guard promised us doesn't include one of those guys."

"You're pretty cute when you get riled. Did you know that?"

"You enjoy teasing and tormenting me, don't you?"

He would enjoy that for a lifetime, given the chance. But it was time to get back to the business of trying to stay alive.

"No comment? You're taking the fifth, aren't you?"

"Gemma, I think this is our ride. We need to plan our next move, you know, what we need to do in Madras."

She glanced at him from the corners of her eyes with a smirky smile painted on those perfect lips. "I suppose I could find some young dude in a nice car and charm him into driving us back to KC's house."

Lex had no claim on Gemma. Why did her joke about flirting with another guy—a young man, not the aging security guard—turn Lex into the green-eyed monster?

A white service truck slowed and stopped beside them. "Heard you two needed a ride to Madras."

The driver of the oversized pickup, a twentysomething man, had his eyes laser focused on Gemma.

Lex leaned toward her and whispered. "Here's your chance. Talk him into taking us to Crooked River Ranch."

She stomped on his toe.

"Yeah." Lex limped toward the truck. "We got stranded on the lake shore. Thanks for helping us out."

Gemma stepped in front of Lex and opened the front door of the king-cab pickup. She slid in beside the driver.

If the eyes of the driver were any indication, Lex had ceased to exist. He slid into the back seat behind Gemma.

"Whereto in Madras?" The driver set his eyes on Gemma and waited.

"Uh." Gemma turned and looked back at Lex. "We probably don't want to go to my place, do we?"

She might have things there that could help them, but her place might also be watched.

"No. Just drop us off at the Safeway," Lex said.

Gemma jabbed a thumb over her shoulder at Lex. "He's a klutz. Fell in the water and ruined his cell."

Lex poked the back of her shoulder.

"No problem," the driver said. "If you need a cell, you need to go to Wal-Mart. I'll take you to the superstore in Redmond."

The wide-eyed look Gemma gave the guy almost got her another poke in the back. "Y'all don't have to carry us all the way to Redmond. That's twenty-five miles out of your way." Her speech was a soft, rich drawl, poured out like molasses from a jug.

The driver's smile spanned the width of his face. "No problem. Glad to do it."

Sure he was. This was not the Gemma that Lex had gotten to know over the last two days. It was a show for Lex's benefit ... or punishment.

"Y'all are so kind. Thank yeeuu." Her Southeastern Texas accent was even getting to Lex, though he knew it was staged.

Lex needed to get his mind back in this game.

The windows of the truck were tinted dark and they wouldn't be stopping in Madras. Those were two pluses to the change of plans. Less chance of being spotted if the black ops team were surveilling Madras.

Lex's soggy wallet had enough cash to buy a cell phone. His first call would be to KC to check on the boys. Beyond that, his plans blurred.

The seemingly intractable problem was how to bring law enforcement in to protect Gemma and Lex without endangering her. There could be BOLOs out, or other information about them. It was too risky to trust local police.

Thirty-five minutes later, when they pulled into the Super Wal-Mart, Lex still had no solution.

Lex opened his door. "Hey, thanks, man."

Gemma slid out and turned to face the driver. "Thank yeeuu so much."

"Anytime. Take care, now." The driver let his eyes linger on Gemma until she closed the door.

The truck rolled away down the parking lot.

"Gemma, was that—"

"Don't even start on me, Lex James. Cuz' if y'all do, I'm fixin' to blow up a storm." She paused. "Now, if you'll be calm, rational and stop accusing me of being Delilah—"

"Don't you mean Scarlett O'Hara?"

"That's enough, Lex. We need to go into the store, buy a phone, and figure out a way to make sure we're still breathing at the end of this day."

"But, Gemma—"

"Is the person you just saw who you think I am?" She pulled him through the door into the store.

"No, but—"

"But nothing. I don't want to hear another word about it. But you *are* kinda' cute when y'all get jealous ... in an obnoxious sort of way."

Lex opened his mouth, then closed it and shook his head.

She grinned and pointed to the other side of the big superstore. "I think the phones are over yooonder."

Someday, if that day ever came and they were still alive, he would get revenge.

Twenty minutes later Lex and Gemma stood outside of the store. Lex had finished setting up the cell phone and reality had returned with all its danger and malevolence.

"Time to call KC."

Gemma nodded. "But, Lex, don't worry her by telling her what we've been through." Her soft drawl replaced her playfulness and the heavy accent.

"I'll have to play that by ear." He keyed in KC's number.

"Hello." Her voice sounded tentative, cautious.

"KC, this is Lex."

"Thank God it's you. Where have you been? I needed to call you but couldn't reach you." The tone in her voice was unlike anything Lex had ever heard from this woman who seemed the master of any situation that came her way.

"Lex, I—"

"KC, I need to tell you what happened. That FBI team, if that's who they really are, chased us down Otter Bench Trail and then down the river. We sort of borrowed a boat, but they flew over in a chopper and blew it up with an RPG."

"Good grief. That's the story that's been playing for the last few hours on the local news stations. Are you both okay?"

"We're okay. Tell you more about it later. We're at the Redmond Wal-Mart. Can you pick us up?"

"Lex …"

The tone of her voice sent a tingling up the back of Lex's neck. "Yeah."

"Two guys broke into my house in the middle of the night. They took Josh and Caleb."

Chapter 17

At 3:30 p.m., Gemma stood beside Lex in the Wal-Mart parking lot.

KC's silver-gray SUV turned in from the street and rolled through the lot toward them.

Gemma couldn't imagine how badly KC must feel. It would be hard for her to face Lex after the boys were kidnapped from her house.

As Gemma stood with her arm curled around Lex's waist, it almost seemed that *her* children had been taken. Josh and Caleb, so full of life, questions, and too smart for their own good, sometimes. No matter how depraved they were, the Fibbies wouldn't hurt the boys, would they?

The driver side window came down as KC's vehicle rolled to a stop beside Gemma and Lex.

"I'm so sorry." KC reached out of the open window and gripped Lex's arm.

KC's arm was scraped and her wrists had been wrapped in bandages.

Gemma leaned in and laid her hand on KC's shoulder. "Are you okay?"

"No!" The eyes of this red-haired, Irish princess flashed anger so intense Gemma took a step back. "We're going to find the boys, rescue them, and I'm going to add some notches to my M4."

Gemma slid into the back seat.

Lex circled the SUV and rode shotgun. "What happened, KC? Did they hurt you?"

"They taped me to a chair. I just got loose about noon and I've been trying to call you since then."

"How were the boys doing when you saw them last?"

KC pulled back onto the street, headed toward northbound Highway 97. "They were calling those men some names that I don't think those thugs understood. The leader of the group told them to be quiet. So they started talking in their own language. Lex, these men want you and Gemma. I don't think they will hurt the boys, intentionally."

"My boys will give them more than they bargained for. But, KC, you didn't know where Gemma and I were, so you couldn't tell them. But did they—"

"They tried to get me to tell them, but it didn't work." KC had spared them the details of her ordeal.

"I'm so sorry, KC." Gemma reached forward and put her hand on KC's shoulder. "Do your wrists—"

"I'm fine, Gemma. It's not the first time I've had a run-in with government black operations."

"No, it isn't," Lex said. "Where's Benjie? They didn't take him, did they?"

"Yesterday evening, I had a premonition, a feeling that something bad was about to happen. I took Benjie to his grandparent's house. They're going to watch him until this is all over. As it turns out, I'm thankful I did that. Who knows what those thugs would have decided. They might have taken him to control me."

"I'm sorry we brought our trouble to you, KC," Lex said.

Gemma clenched her teeth as anger flashed white hot. "Until someone cleans house in that blasted DOJ, so it can live up to its name again, *every* American is in trouble."

"But not like you and Lex," KC said as she drove around the loop and onto the ramp for 97 north.

Lex stared at the dash with a look so intense he might burn a hole in it. "KC, will you drop me off at the Otter

Bench trailhead to see if my car is still where we left it yesterday?"

"Sure. But you might want to check it out for any booby traps before you drive it."

"We took off in such a hurry, them chasing us down the trail, that I doubt they had much time to think about bombs and such. They were pretty intent on just shooting us."

"They almost did," Gemma added.

KC accelerated to highway speed and merged into the traffic on 97. "Are you a runner, Gemma?"

"Used to be in high school."

"That probably saved your and Lex's lives."

"She ran me into the ground," Lex said. "Do you have any idea where they might have taken the boys?"

"Let's get your car and then meet at my place to strategize about the twins."

Gemma made a mental note. KC had avoided Lex's question. "We've been calling them the Fibbies. They don't deserve to be called FBI."

Gemma snorted her disgust at those who would violate their sacred oath to defend the Constitution and the American people. What did they call it, the United States Uniformed Services Oath? "They promised to defend the Constitution and to faithfully discharge their duties. This group is a bunch of liars and—" She had started to add murderers, but she couldn't say that in front of Lex after these men had taken his boys. "Well, that's why we call them Fibbies."

KC pulled into the right lane and accelerated to well above the speed limit. "There were two Fibbies. There are three of us. The odds are in our favor.

"There was a third one whom they left at Opal Springs to watch for us. That makes three."

"Okay. The odds are even. They will have to call my landline to start negotiating for whatever they want."

"They want me." Gemma's stomach churned now. Full-fledged nausea. She was to blame for Lex's boys being in danger and for what had happened to KC. Somehow, Gemma needed to bring it all to an end. But, with Lex involved, something that was also her fault, resolving the situation had grown more complicated. If there were some way she could free the boys ...

It grew quiet in KC's SUV until they had turned off at Terrebonne and driven to Crooked River Ranch. KC descended the steep hill to the ranch plateau and continued north to the trailhead.

The route seemed unfamiliar to Gemma. When she and Lex had taken it yesterday, they had been chased and shot at.

In a couple of minutes, she sighted Lex's SUV on the loop at the end of the road.

Someone had closed the doors they had flung open when they started their run. Had those men left any other surprises, like the ones KC mentioned?

KC stopped about fifty yards from Lex's vehicle. "Check your SUV, Lex. Look for any magnetic devices underneath the dash and underneath the vehicle."

Lex opened his door.

Gemma reached forward and clamped a hand on his shoulder. "Lex ... please be careful. I ..."

"I will be, Gemma." He held her gaze for a moment, then got out of KC's SUV and walked slowly toward his.

KC had studied Lex and Gemma's interaction and gave Gemma a long look that seemed to say KC knew something was happening between Lex and Gemma. But KC didn't comment.

After five minutes of crawling under the vehicle, looking inside and under the hood, Lex dusted himself off and walked back to KC's SUV. "It looks fine. No unexpected gifts or signs of tampering. But the tank was low when we left it yesterday. I think I'll drive back to Terrebonne and gas up. Meet you two back at KC's in a half hour or so."

"But we're staying here until you're driving away safely, right KC?"

"Of course we are," KC said.

Gemma prayed as Lex walked toward his SUV, keys in hand. She prayed it wouldn't blow up, that Lex would be kept safe, and that she would discover some way to make sure those boys came home safely to Lex, even if it cost Gemma Saint everything.

Five minutes later, after Lex drove safely away toward Terrebonne, two-thirds of Gemma's prayer had been answered.

She would now work on the third part of her request.

KC pulled into her garage, closed the garage door, and they both got out.

"Gemma, I'm going to check to see if I got any phone calls. At some point, your Fibbies are going to call because that's the only way they can reach Lex to make their demands."

Gemma followed her into the house and waited as KC checked the phone in the kitchen.

"No calls yet."

"KC, once they call, they will be calling the shots and we'll be responding. They'll be on offense and we'll be on defense. But if we could locate them before they call—did they leave any clues about where they were taking the boys?"

"Maybe. I didn't want to mention it to Lex until we had time to think about it with clear heads. You know, so we could come up with a plan that didn't put Josh and Caleb in more danger."

Gemma was formulating her own plan to keep the boys and Lex safe, but she needed more information from KC. "So you saw or heard something when the men were here?"

KC walked into the living room and pointed to a hallway that appeared to lead to the bedrooms. "I struggled with two of them here, before they got me tied and taped into a chair in the study. After I got free ..." She pointed down the hallway. "... I found a business card on the floor near where I had fought with one of the men. The card was from a property manager in Sisters. The card had a phone number written in pencil on the back. Just before you called, I looked up the phone number online. For a couple of bucks you can get the address if you have the landline phone number."

Maybe this was the chance Gemma had prayed for. "You mean you might know where the boys are?"

"Like I said, maybe. The address traced to a vacation rental house out in the boonies north of Sisters, and that property is managed by the person on the card. I'd bet good money that's where they have the boys."

KC's eyes widened when the phone rang. "This might be those men. I hope it isn't, but I need to answer. We don't want them getting impatient and doing something rash."

"Kidnapping two little boys is rash, if you ask me." And Gemma's plan might be considered rash too. But if it worked ...

KC strode through the living room and headed toward kitchen.

When she moved out of sight, Gemma hurried into study.

A laptop computer with a mouse attached sat on a desk in the study. A printer sat on one corner of the desk.

Gemma wiggled the mouse and the screensaver ended, leaving an open web browser on the display. Maybe she was in luck.

She clicked to view the browser's recent history and saw a link to a map. Gemma clicked on the link and got a map showing a house with a red icon. She sent a screen print to the default printer and the printer on the desk came to life.

She tried another link and saw the phone number of the house.

Gemma took the printed map, found a pen on the desk and wrote the phone number on the map. She took a blank sheet of paper from the printer, folded the map and the blank paper, and slipped the papers and the pen into the pocket of her shorts.

She hurried back into the hallway and walked toward the living room.

What had only been a remote possibility now became an actionable plan.

If Gemma got the opportunity to drive away by herself, she could surprise the kidnappers. Then she could offer herself to free the boys, and convince the kidnappers that Lex knew nothing of consequence about the conspiracy.

If she could accomplish that, her plan might work, and Gemma could sacrifice herself to save the people she had endangered. Maybe Gemma's jinx would end today.

But one problem remained. She must not let Lex know what she was doing. In fact, she must distract Lex completely, so he wouldn't follow her.

Gemma had to make Lex not want to follow her. That meant lying to him about her feelings for him. She needed to give him a message so strong and so painful that Lex would loathe her. Hurting him was the only way. Otherwise, he would follow her.

Only one thought came to mind. She must make Lex think she was another Melissa.

KC walked into the living room.

"KC, was it them?"

"No. And I'm glad. I wasn't prepared to talk to them. Not until we talk to Lex."

"I'm going to use your bathroom down the hall, if that's okay."

"Whatever you need, Gemma, feel free."

Gemma nodded, walked down the hall and into the bathroom. She closed and locked the door, took out the blank paper from her pocket, along with the pen, and sought words that would paint Gemma Saint as another Melissa in the life of Lex James.

Chapter 18

4:00 p.m. near Sisters, Oregon

A soft alarm sounded on Blade's cell. He accessed the app that had opened.

The tracker Blade had carefully hidden on Lex's SUV had sent a signal indicating the SUV was moving.

Had James survived the RPG from the chopper, or was someone else driving his SUV? On the remote chance that it was Lex driving that vehicle, Blade needed to find it. If it was Lex, they could take him out and either wait for Gemma Saint to surface or, perhaps the boys might lure in Ms. Saint. If both James and Saint were in the SUV, Blade's mission would soon be over.

"Come on, Walker. James's SUV is on the move. You and I need to see who's driving. Kirby, watch those boys. Keep them locked in the master bedroom. It has a bathroom so they don't need to be let out. Check on them a couple of times each hour to make sure they don't get into mischief."

"Got it covered, boss," Kirby said.

Walker had already gone out the front door of the house and headed toward their van. "You driving, Blade?"

"Yes. But see if you can get some local news. I want to hear what they're saying about the helicopter incident."

Walker tuned in to a local news station. After they reached Highway 126 near Sisters, the news station had a breaking news alert. A reporter was going to interview a witness who had some new information to share.

"To this time, no bodies have been found, so speculation continues about the fate of the driver of the boat. The boat owner said two people stole the boat at the mouth of the Crooked River. Mr. Thompson, please, tell us what you saw at about 2:30 p.m. today."

"Well, I got a call from security at Round Butte Dam saying that a man and a young woman had wandered into the restricted area around the dam. They said they'd been stranded on the lake shore and tried to walk out. And they hadn't intended to violate the restricted area. Security cleared them and asked me to give them a ride to Madras."

"Did you take them to Madras?"

"Well, the man's cell phone had gotten wet. They needed a phone. I suggested Wal-Mart. So I drove them to the superstore in Redmond."

"Can you describe the two, so our listeners can be on the lookout?"

"Yes. But why? They didn't look dangerous, and the young lady, she was something else. About five-foot-six. Long, curly dark hair. And big brown eyes. Except for her wet, wrinkled clothes, she might have walked off a Hollywood movie set."

"Gemma Saint!" Blade cursed her and whatever guardian angel had kept her alive three or more times when most people would be in a morgue by now.

"Quiet, Blade. He's talking about the man."

"... about six-foot-two. Short, dark hair. Athletic looking. I'm not sure, but I think his eyes were blue."

"That's Lex James, Blade. After Drake's report, I don't know how that's possible, but they're out there, loose in the wild," Walker said.

"But we still have our ace-in-the-hole ... Lex James's twins."

Blade's cell rang. He pulled it out and glanced at the caller ID. "Great. That's really great. It's Max Carr calling for status."

"You're driving. You want me to take it, Blade?"

"No. I need to do some fancy footwork. I know Carr better than you. I'll handle it."

Blade picked up the call and pressed the phone to his ear. "Sikes."

"Carr here. You were supposed to give me status before this. What's up, Blade?"

"Plan A and B are running in parallel. B is on track. But we had a shot at James and Saint. Took it and—"

"You didn't get them, did you? What is it with you and your team?"

"Don't you want to hear what happened?"

"No, I'm sure I don't. But I suppose I need to hear it anyway."

"We caught the two in a boat on the lake. Called in Drake and the chopper crew. They blew the boat up with an RPG. We used the SMAW. The boat was scattered all over the lake. I don't know how, but Lex James and Gemma Saint survived, apparently with nothing more than a dip in the lake."

"Now that you've squandered any further use of the chopper, what are the plans?"

"I just located James using a tracker I put on his car. We're headed to intercept him now. Either we'll get James or both of them in a few minutes. As security, we have James's twins."

"How do the twins help if you get James but not the girl?"

"All indications are James and Ms. Saint are getting pretty tight. His twin boys might bring Gemma Saint to us."

"If you believe that, Sikes, you're a fool. When a person's life is on the line, a stranger's kids don't mean anything to them."

"I'm not sure about that. Both Saint and James call themselves Christians."

Carr laughed. "Then you're about to see just how big a hypocrite most Christians are. Jesus supposedly gave his life for them. Ms. Saint wont' reciprocate for someone else's twin boys no matter how cute they are."

"In about fifteen minutes, we'll take out whoever's in that SUV. But, to make that happen, I need to get off this call and take a short cut through some back roads."

"Okay, I'll let you go. But, Sikes, I'm warning you, if this attempt fails, or if you get Lex James but not Gemma Saint, I'm going to pull you from this mission. Then you'll find your career going to blazes in a basket. Do you understand?"

"I heard you, Carr." Blade ended the call and glanced at Walker.

Walker nodded. "I heard most of it. If Carr pulls our team, we can say goodbye to our cushy DC assignments, complete with all those delightful perks."

"If we catch that SUV, everything will work out fine."

"Uh ... Blade, the GPS display on the van just went flakey."

"You sure?"

"Look at it. It's showing gibberish."

"Turn it off then back on."

"I already tried that."

Blade swore at the defective device. "Do you remember which roads go through to Crooked River Ranch or Lower Bridge Road?"

"No," Walker said. "You were driving when we came through here."

"Great. I'll have to try to navigate this maze of roads using that crude map on the tracking app. Here, Walker, take it and guide me through to where that SUV is headed."

"It looks like Mr. James is going to Terrebonne."

"Then get me there, Walker. When we catch Mr. James, use your M4 and don't be particular about who you shoot. We can't let anyone in that SUV survive."

Chapter 19

The bathroom clock said 4:30 p.m.

Gemma stood at the bathroom counter and read her note one more time to make sure she'd said what she needed to tell Lex.

A car drove up and stopped in front of KC's house.

Lex.

She signed the note and wiped the tears from her eyes. If there were only some other way to sacrifice herself without hurting Lex. He had been hurt enough already—losing his sister, then losing the woman who might have helped him raise the twins. And now, the boys were in danger.

Lex might never find happiness after reading this note. But he could be a good father to Josh and Caleb. He already had been, and he hadn't needed Gemma Saint's help to do that. He would be fine. And the disasters that followed her would no longer bother Lex and the twins.

Gemma studied her face in the bathroom mirror then washed all the tear tracks from her cheeks. She couldn't do anything about her red eyes, so she painted a smile on her face and left the bathroom just as the front door opened.

She walked down the hallway toward the living room, where Lex and KC stood.

Gemma met KC's gaze. "Did they call yet?"

KC shook her head.

What would KC would say next? It could impact Gemma's plan.

118

"Lex, we do have one clue about where they took the boys."

"Then we need to go, now. Where are they, KC?"

"What do you plan to do? Just walk in and let them kill you? That won't help Josh and Caleb. We need a plan before we go anywhere."

"Okay. Show me where this place is."

"It's out in the country not too far from Sisters. I have a map." KC turned and headed into the kitchen.

Lex followed.

Gemma stopped at the edge of the kitchen.

KC spread a printed map out on the kitchen table. "We need to decide what we want to accomplish. Then we'll take an inventory of the weapons we have and come up with a plan that makes sense. First, do you think we should call for help from law enforcement?"

Lex shook his head. "If we call the wrong person, it's all over. Remember, these guys are FBI agents. They can show their badges and bluff the police. Maybe bluff us right into their custody and get local police's blessing on the whole procedure."

"If we take them on, I still have my M4 from several years ago. It's military issue. The first time we shoot, they won't be expecting automatic weapon fire. That may surprise them and give us a momentary edge."

"That's great, KC."

"Lex, like you said, these are FBI agents. It won't be like a shooting gallery. They shoot back and they have your boys."

If they went through with a plan to attack the Fibbies, it could go badly. But, if Lex had left the keys in his car, this was Gemma's chance. She had nothing to contribute to the plan, but maybe she could make the plan unnecessary. "Excuse me. I'll be right back."

She could feel KC's eyes on her back as Gemma walked into the living room.

Please. Don't let KC suspect anything.

"Gemma's been really down since she heard about the boys. Probably blaming herself." KC spoke softly, but not softly enough.

Gemma angled toward the hallway leading to the bathroom. She left the note on the counter and walked softly back to the living room.

While KC and Lex studied the map, Gemma slipped quietly out the front door.

Lex's keys were in the ignition.

She opened the car door and slid into the driver's seat. Once she started the car, they might come to stop her. But if she didn't rev the engine, they may not hear from the kitchen, especially if the two were engrossed in the map and their plan.

Gemma buckled in and hit the ignition.

The engine started more quietly than she anticipated. Gemma slipped the transmission into gear and drove slowly around the circle drive to the street.

She turned onto Rim Road and, in a couple of minutes, turned onto Chinook Drive. As she approached Terrebonne-Lower Bridge Road, she turned into a pull-out and took the map from her pocket. She unfolded the page, got her bearings and memorized the route she would take to the house near Sisters.

If she could get the men to release the boys while Gemma surrendered, Josh and Caleb could hide in the woods until Lex and KC arrived.

Once Lex and KC noticed Gemma was gone, they would come quickly, plan or no plan.

The boys were smart, they would know what to do if Gemma could tell them Lex was coming soon. But what if she couldn't get that message to them without being overheard? And how could she be sure the boys got away before the men took Gemma?

No matter how it turned out. Lex would be better off. He and KC would have at least one less person to try to keep safe. Because Gemma Saint would be dead.

Chapter 20

Blade stopped at the intersection of two country roads somewhere northeast of Sisters. He had been driving for fifteen minutes and feared he had lost too much time to catch James's SUV.

"Walker, where are we?"

"Right where you wanted to be. Lower Bridge Way straight ahead."

"I said Lower Bridge *Road*."

"This blasted app keeps changing the map display. You can't zoom in and pan around. You can't find anything."

"Then just keep tracking the SUV. Where is it now?"

"After it stopped along Highway 97 in Terrebonne, it went back to Crooked River Ranch—to the rim above it."

"That's KC Daniels' place. Tell me if it leaves."

Blade made a U-turn and backtracked for a half mile. "What happened to Lower Bridge Way? The sign just said this is Lambert Road."

"That may not be a bad thing, Blade. If you stay on this road for about two miles, you should come to Lower Bridge Road near the bridge over the Deschutes."

"Well, we're not lost anymore, but we're losing time. If we can get to Daniels' house before that SUV leaves, we won't need those kids. I'm betting Mr. James and Ms. Saint are paying KC Daniels a visit. I think we should pay them one too."

"If they're all there and we start shooting, what do we do about Daniels?"

"What do you think? We don't shoot her."

"Blade, you've heard about her. What if she starts shooting back? If we kill her too, you know, all three of them together, some local detective is going to put two and two together and this whole thing could backfire. Carr would have a cow."

"No, Walker. In that case Carr would have a cell in Leavenworth. But we would retire in South America."

"Uh ... I don't think we have to worry about that." Walker's eyes had locked on the cell phone in his hands.

"What do you see, Walker?"

"The SUV just left Daniels' house. It looks like it's headed back to Lower Bridge Road."

Blade pushed the accelerator to the floor. "Tell me which way it turns when it gets there."

In a couple of minutes, the Deschutes River became visible in a canyon below them.

"This app must have hiccupped or something. The SUV fast forwarded and is now headed west on Lower Bridge Road. Do you think it's going to Sisters?"

"One thing I do know," Blade said. "If I can get to Lower Bridge Road first, we'll see it go by and possibly we'll see who's in it."

Why would Lex James be going toward Sisters? Did he know about their safe house? That thought troubled Blade in a dozen different ways.

He accelerated to fifty, but it was too fast for the small road. He backed off on the accelerator.

"It just passed Lambert," Walker said. "How could they possibly know where our safe house is?"

"KC Daniels. She was a world-class hacker. Used to protect defense networks in DC. She's caused trouble ever since she got involved."

"Blade, that woman killed part of a contingent of Army Rangers, a black ops team."

"I guess I didn't hear that part. You mean a team like us?"

"No, a team of special forces. A lot better than us."

Blade braked to a stop at Lower Bridge Road. "Then I've got one question for you. Who do you suppose is in that SUV?"

Walker looked up from the app display. "Maybe you should add ... and what are they packing?"

Chapter 21

Where was Gemma?

"KC, isn't Gemma in the bathroom?" Lex said.

"Yeah. Second time in about fifteen minutes. She's upset."

"I'm going to check on her. Something's not right."

Lex walked through the living room and down the hallway.

The bathroom door stood open.

He looked in and saw what looked like a note on the bathroom counter.

Reality hit Lex like a blow to his solar plexus. "KC, I think Gemma's gone."

KC's footsteps sounded from the living room then stopped.

Lex picked up the note and started to read it.

KC's rapid steps echoed from the hallway. "Your SUV's gone, Lex."

Another punch to Lex's gut.

"She left a note." The knot in Lex's stomach tightened.

Lex,

I have brought you, the boys, and KC so much trouble that the best thing for everyone is for me to disappear—to go someplace where I will never be found. Don't look for me. I need to stay hidden, indefinitely. You won't see me again. That is as it should be.

Lex, I took your SUV but will leave it where you can find it. Thanks for helping me escape the FBI thugs. I'm not sure I could have done that on my own.

While we were on the run, I said some things and did some things that I should not have done or said. Even if there was no danger, it would be best for me to leave now. I was never meant to be a wife and certainly not a mother.

I wish you well with your business. Feel free to break my story. You know enough of it to alert the people of this nation to the truth about government corruption.

Goodbye, Lex.

Gemma

When Lex finished the note, he realized KC's heavy breathing came from over his shoulder. Now she knew the truth about Gemma, too.

Gemma was like all the women he'd ever known. He should never have trusted her. Never have fallen for her. And she had probably broken the boys' hearts too. They had seen their mother in Gemma. Then she left, stealing every bit of joy she had brought and more. Then she stole his SUV.

"Gemma, Melissa—they're all the same."

"What in heaven's name are you talking about, Lex James? Let me see that note. I didn't get to finish reading it."

Lex flung it at her.

KC snatched it out of the air, before it floated to the floor. She focused on the note. "Oh, man. Oh, woman. Lex, this thing is full of lies. Can't you see what she's—"

"Oh, I see it alright. Gemma is the return of Melissa. The only difference is Melissa didn't even leave a note. I should have seen this coming. How could I be so—"

"Stop it right now, Mr. James!"

"Why?"

"Just answer this question. When did Gemma ever mention marrying you—even the remote possibility of that—or mention being a mother to your boys?"

He didn't reply.

"When, Lex?" KC's eyes bored into him. Her nostrils flared with each breath. She had clenched both fists.

Lex backed away before one of those fists found his face.

"What happened to your Melissa accusations? Is the truth starting to jell in that mushy head of yours?"

Lex looked away from KC's fiery face and tried to concentrate. "She—she didn't."

"Then why did she mention them in this note, a note obviously intended to be her final communication with you?"

"Evidently, she wanted her words to be hurtful."

KC nodded slowly. "Maybe. But if she hadn't thought about being your wife and Josh's and Caleb's mother, she wouldn't have thought to put it in the note."

"I—"

"Don't bother answering that. Try this instead. Where do you think Gemma is going? Tell me what you really believe. Not what's in that thick skull of yours but what's in your heart."

"I don't know."

"Come on. You've seen her in action when danger threatened her. Was she so terrified that she thought only of herself? What would the Gemma you've come to know over the last two days do?"

"I don't think I really knew her."

"If you were Gemma, and you had brought danger to a family, then its children were kidnapped, how would you feel? And if you thought you could sacrifice yourself to save the kids, what would you do?

"I wouldn't leave a note that—"

"Be honest, Lex. Keep your emotions and Melissa out of it. What would you do?"

"I'd probably try something to free the kids."

The truth came with a lightning flash of insight followed by a thunderclap that shook Lex to his core. "We've got to stop her, KC."

"Lex James just got his two hundred back. Follow me into the study. I've got an idea."

Lex wanted to bolt and run to the door. But he had no vehicle outside and had no idea where he would drive it if it was there. He followed KC into the study, while his heart played a percussion solo in his chest.

"She was on my laptop. Let me see what she was up to." KC opened her browser and restored its open tabs.

"Darn. She accessed the map of the place I thought those men may have taken the boys. Let me look at the applications log."

KC clicked a couple of times with the mouse and waited for a window that opened and eventually filled with information. "Gemma printed the map. Using my history, she pulled up the phone number I used in my search. She has a map to the house and the landline phone number for it. So what do you think she's up to, Lex?"

"She's going to try to trade herself for Josh and Caleb. I'm not completely stupid, KC."

"But you're pretty doggoned close." KC sent something to the printer and it fed a sheet of paper through to the output bin.

Lex turned to leave the study. "We've got to stop her."

"First, we need a plan. A new one. We can't take off half-cocked and get her and us killed. That wouldn't help the boys."

KC's phone rang.

"Great timing." She shook her head. "I've got to get this. It could be them."

KC picked up the phone in the study. "Hello ... I'm not sure I should answer that." KC nodded to Lex.

It was the kidnappers.

KC wrote something on a sheet of paper. "Got it. You want me to repeat after you ... Okay ... This is a message for Lex James ... He is to come to the address you gave me and exchange himself for his two boys ... Be there in one hour or bad things will happen."

"He hung up, Lex. But you got the gist of the message."

Lex nodded.

"They didn't mention Gemma. That means she hasn't had time to get there. But this is going to get really sticky when she shows up."

"They want me as badly as they want Gemma. When she arrives, they'll kill her and keep the boys as bait for me. When I take the bait, they'll kill me and, when they realize how bright the boys are, they'll kill them too."

Chapter 22

Josh tried the bedroom door after the man called Kirby left.

Kirby wasn't real smart, but he didn't forget. He'd locked the door.

But they could get away if he and Cabe both used their two hundred. Somehow, they could do it. They always came up with a way to do stuff.

"Cabe, remember what Uncalex told us about why Mama and Dad called us Joshua and Caleb?"

"Yeah," Caleb said. "They were the good spies. They weren't afraid of those giants. Joshua and Caleb said if we follow God, He'll lead us. And we don't hafta' be afraid of our emenies, 'cause we can eat'em alive."

Sometimes Caleb went a little crazy when he told stories. This was a Bible story, so it needed to be told right. "I think they said devour. It's like eat, but it means more like gobble up."

"But we can do this, right?" Caleb said.

"Yeah. And we don't hafta' tear our clothes."

"I think they ripped their clothes 'cause they were mad."

Josh shook his head. "I'm not mad. Only a little bit scared."

"But Joshua said don't be afraid of'em."

God said that a lot of times in the Bible, but it didn't always help Josh. He still got scared of stuff, sometimes. "I wouldn't be afraid, Cabe, if I knew how we were gonna get'em? Kirby took out all of the stuff we could hurt'em with."

"I got my squirt gun."

"Cabe, they took all the water out of it. It wouldn't help anyway."

"Maybe we can fill it with something really bad. Something dangerous."

He couldn't let Cabe try to act out one of his crazy stories. "That's not a good idea. First let's look for something that's gonna work."

"Okay. You check the closet, Josh, and I'll look in the bathroom."

Josh looked through the closet and spied one golf club leaning against the back wall. Good thing some hanging stuff hid it or Kirby would've taken it too.

He took the club in his hand. It would hurt somebody. But if they just tried to hit him, a big man like Kirby would probably just take it away and hit them with it.

Cabe's voice came from the bathroom. "Josh, come and look what I found under the sink."

Josh ran to the bathroom door and looked at the bottle in Cabe's hand. "Toilet bowl cleaner? We're not trying clean 'em up, Cabe."

"Somebody needs to clean up their mouths. They're always talkin' about that stuff floatin' in the toilet bowl."

"Yeah. I wonder if their mamas ever washed their mouth out with soap."

"They shoulda'. But soap's not strong enough for what we need. We need something that really hurts."

Cabe grinned. "Yeah, that's why I read the warning on the bottle. It's got bleach."

"Ya' mean that stuff Uncalex ruined our jeans with?"

"Yeah. That stuff," Cabe said. "But ya' know something? The people that own this house really gotta be stupid."

"Right. Only stupid people would leave poison stuff with bleach where little kids like us could get it." Josh laughed until he snorted. "But listen to what it says on the bottle. Danger: Causes irreparable damage to eyes."

"Josh, what does repurble mean?"

"Means you can't fix'em."

"So he'll be blind?"

Josh shrugged. "Or maybe he just can't see very well. But they can probably fix his eyes while he's in jail. I know it's bad, Cabe. But we gotta do it anyway. It's all we have, and these people want to hurt Uncalex and Gemma."

"Let's use it. But we gotta wait and see if they leave Kirby alone in the house. Cause I can only squirt one guy before they get us. That Blade guy said he and Walker were going somewhere. If they go, we can try it on Kirby."

Josh looked down at the floor and shook his head. "If we miss his eyes, ya' know what's gonna happen?"

Cabe grabbed his shirt and yanked. "He'll tear his clothes off like those people in the Bible."

"Nope. He'll probly tear our heads off."

"Then I have to get both eyes, so he can't see."

"You're a purty good shot with your squirt gun, Cabe. But you gotta make sure ya' don't miss, because—"

"Cause if I miss, we're toast."

Josh carried the bedroom chair to the door. "Hear the motor? The car's leavin'. We gotta get ready."

"I'll fill my squirt gun."

By the time Josh adjusted the chair by the door, Cabe was back with his squirt gun. It wasn't light yellow anymore. It had turned a weird blue-green color. "If you stand on the chair, your squirt gun will be even with Kirby's eyes."

"How do you know that?"

"I looked where his head poked in last time he checked on us. You gotta remember stuff like that, Cabe, 'cause you never know when you might need it."

Cabe climbed up in the chair and stood. "Am I up high enough?"

"Looks perfect. But stay back until he pokes his head in. Then ya' gotta shoot fast before he knows you're there. Ready, Cabe?"

"I don't know?"

"I thought you said we're gonna eat our emenies alive and that God would protect us."

"Yeah. And God doesn't lie, so ... I guess I'm ready."

"One more thing," Josh said, "Don't let him get his hands on ya', Cabe. Just a minute."

Josh went to the closet and pulled out the golf club. "I saw this in the closet when you found the toilet bowl cleaner. If Kirby grabs one of us, the other one should hit him in the head with this."

"What number does it have on it?"

"It doesn't matter, Cabe. It's gonna hurt."

"But what number is it?"

"It doesn't have a number. It says SW. I'm gonna lean it up by the door. Are we ready?"

"Yeah."

Josh beat on door and yelled, "Caleb is sick! Help us! He's pukin' all over the bed." He listened.

Nothing.

He pounded with his fist and yelled again, "Oh, gross! He's really sick now!"

Footsteps clomped down the hallway.

"Get ready, Cabe. Shoot fast."

If this didn't work, it would be worse than the time they opened Melissa's purse in church and had an accident with her pepper stuff. Kirby would be a lot madder than the pastor was when he had to stop the church service. Maybe as mad as Melissa.

The door knob clicked.

Josh stepped back.

The door opened, and Kirby poked his head in.

Cabe's squirt gun shot a lot with each squirt. He shoved it in Kirby's face and shot one long squirt that went across both eyes.

Kirby's eyes turned purple and he screamed. Then he put his hands over his eyes and his potty mouth started. Somebody needed to flush it.

Cabe took care of it. When Kirby screamed again, Cabe got him in the mouth. That was a good place for toilet bowl cleaner.

Josh grabbed the golf club and watched Kirby.

But Kirby must have sucked in some of that yucky stuff, because he bent over and hacked and choked.

Then he tried to grab Cabe. But Kirby's eyes were closed and Cabe had already jumped off the chair. But Kirby almost caught him.

Josh needed to stop Kirby before those grabbing hands got one of them.

Josh moved beside Kirby and swung the SW club as hard as he could.

It hit Kirby's shin. He fell on the floor with one hand holding his leg and the other over his eyes.

It was awful what they did to Kirby. But they had to do it. Cause what Kirby would do to them was even awfuller.

Kirby was out of the doorway now, crawling toward the bathroom door.

When he got to the bathroom, he got up and started the water running in the sink.

Caleb slid his squirt gun along the floor. It went under the bed. "Wouldn't want him to use it on us."

Josh did the same with the golf club. "Can't take this with us. Let's go before he washes his eyes out."

Josh grabbed Caleb's hand and they ran down the hall to the garage door.

"Remember the doggie door we saw when they brought us in?"

"Yeah. It's big. We can crawl through."

"Cabe, when we get through it, we have to run so far into the woods they can never find us. Cause if we don't …"

Cabe's head went through door. "I know. We're toast."

Josh shoved on Caleb's fanny then crawled through behind him.

Outside the garage, Josh pointed to where the most trees grew and they both ran toward the woods.

The sound of a car came through the trees. Not close to the house. It was way up the driveway.

"This way, Cabe. We need to see who this is. But don't let anybody see you. It might be Blade."

"It's Uncalex's car. What's he coming here for?"

The car parked too far away to see who was in it.

Josh grabbed the back of Cabe's shirt. "Don't just run to it. We better see who's in it first."

Josh started moving through trees, circling to the other side of the house.

"Cabe, it's Gemma," Josh whispered. "Listen, she's yelling at Kirby."

"If you let the boys go, you can have me instead."

"Oh, no. This is real bad. She doesn't know we got away."

"You give yourself up first, then we'll release the boys." That was Kirby's voice. But he wasn't gonna let Gemma see him.

"Do ya' think Kirby can see anything now?" Cabe asked.

"I don't know, but Kirby's bluffin'. He can't see much. We need to warn Gemma before they get her."

"Kirby can't get her. He probly can't even see her," Caleb said.

"Cabe, listen. Another car's comin' down the driveway."

"Josh, it's that black car they took us in. Look. It stopped behind Gemma's car, and Blade's driving it."

"What are we gonna do, Cabe?"

"I don't know, but we can't let them see us or we're toast."

"If Kirby ever catches us we'll be burned toast."

"And they won't treat us like little kids anymore, cause now they know we're dangerous."

"But, Cabe ... somehow we gotta' save Gemma. No matter what. Or she won't ever get to be our mama."

Chapter 23

Blade stopped the van thirty or forty yards behind the SUV parked ahead of them.

He slid down the driver's side window and listened. "Gemma Saint found our safe house and she's dialoguing with Kirby? This looks easy, but something's not right."

"You got that right," Walker said. "We've got the boys to lure Lex James, so Kirby should have made Saint Gemma a martyr by now. Surely he's smart enough to figure that out."

"I don't know about that. His IQ's probably not as high as today's temperature. You wait here and make sure she doesn't get away. I'm going to circle the house and get inside. We need to know what's up with Kirby. This is the second time he's screwed up in two days."

Two minutes later, Blade entered the house from the back door.

Ms. Saint and Kirby were still arguing about who was going to do what. This was crazy. Kirby should already have her tied up inside the house or have shot her.

Blade strode through the kitchen and stopped in the doorway to the living room.

Kirby had the front door open only a crack. He didn't have his gun and he kept rubbing his eyes.

"Kirby, what in blazes do you think you're doing?"

Kirby turned toward Blade. "Blade, is that you?"

"Of course it's me. What's that blue stuff all over your face?"

"Those twins. They're two little demons. They—"

"You let them get away, didn't you?" If he had let them escape, Kirby's usefulness would end. Perhaps Kirby's life would also.

"They can't have gone far, Blade. But before I could chase them down, Gemma Saint drove up and started negotiating for the boys. She doesn't know they slipped out."

"Slipped out? Two little boys, only four, are slippery? Does this have something to do with those blue streaks on your face?" Blade pulled out his phone. "Don't answer that just yet."

He hit Walker's number and waited.

"Hey, what's up in the house, Blade?"

"You're not going to believe this. Kirby let the twins get away. They're somewhere in the trees near the house. I'll find them. You just get Ms. Saint. She's not armed."

"Are you sure of that?"

"Are you saying you can't handle a sweet, little saint of a girl? Just get her, Walker, and bring her to the house. I've got some questions for her, before we reduce the scope of this mission."

"You mean reduce it down to Lex James?"

"Yes. But if those two infantile delinquents are as smart as I'm beginning to think, we might have to throw them in on the deal too."

Chapter 24

Gemma had parked Lex's SUV about seventy-five yards from the house on its long driveway.

A man had stuck his head out of the door and asked who she was. Didn't these guys know Gemma Saint? Surely they must have pictures of her.

"If you let the boys go, you can have me instead."

"You give yourself up first, then we'll release the boys."

Maybe she needed to be more explicit. "I'm willing to trade Gemma Saint for the James twins. But I have to know that they are safe and unharmed before these negotiations go any further."

"They're safe and they're okay." The man seemed terribly distracted for an FBI agent supposedly holding kidnapped boys. He kept blinking his eyes and, she couldn't see him well, but there appeared to be something wrong with his face.

The birds in the forest had stopped singing, except for the raspy chatter of a magpie.

Not a good sign.

Gemma scanned the trees on her right and left, looking for any movement.

"Put your hands on your head." The voice of a man behind her.

Gemma tried to turn around.

"Don't turn ... or you won't like what happens, Ms. Saint."

It was one of the Fibbies. Gemma had blown it. Was this more of Gemma's jinx?

Maybe not. Maybe she needed to be inside that house to help the boys. Since this Fibbie didn't shoot her on sight, she would probably be inside in a few moments.

Gemma needed to see those twins, now. She needed to know they were safe. But she had lost her bargaining power to free them. Now, she needed another plan to spring Josh and Caleb. She couldn't create a plan until she saw what she was up against inside the house.

What felt like the barrel of a gun prodded her back. "Keep your hands on your head and walk slowly toward the house."

When they reached the house, the front door opened and their leader, a man Gemma had seen near Opal Springs, waved her inside.

"Here she is, Blade."

"Welcome, Ms. Saint. It's so nice of you to drop by for a visit."

"Where are the boys? I want to see them now."

Blade poked his finger at her chest. "A person in your position doesn't have the right to want anything."

Gemma glared at Blade. He needed to know she wasn't afraid of him no matter what he did or threatened.

She had a Heavenly Father who filtered everything before it got to Gemma. He didn't stop all evil in this present age but, one day, justice would prevail, and that wouldn't require some corrupt politicians in a corrupt Department of Justice or thugs like Blade trying to carry out their plans.

Blade glared back at Gemma, then appeared to study her eyes. "You know, with an attitude like that, you're dangerous. Walker, zip-tie her wrists and ankles. If any other unexpected visitors show up, duct tape her mouth. We wouldn't want our little saint yelling out obscenities or, perhaps, warnings."

"My vision's still blurry and it's not clearing up. Blade, I need to see a doctor."

Blade faced the complainer and put his hands on his hips. "Blurry? Kirby, my knowledge is a little blurry. Suppose you tell us exactly what happened when those two forty-five-pound giants took you out."

Out? Had the boys gotten away?

"It was your fault, Blade." Kirby's voice had turned raspy and whining. "You let that little twerp keep his gun."

"Yeah, I did. His *squirt* gun."

"But they filled it with ..."

"Well, let's hear it. With Kryptonite?"

"With ... toilet bowl cleaner."

Blade raised his eyebrows.

Gemma laughed.

Blade shot her a threatening glance. "That's enough from the saint in the choir loft. Continue, Kirby."

"When I stuck my head in to check on them—"

"They shot you with their squirt gun. Give the man a purple heart. He's already got a purple eye." Blade paused. "If your vision is permanently damaged, you have no one to blame but yourself and your own stupidity. I can't sympathize with an idiot who could let a couple of preschoolers get away and blind him in the process. You call yourself an FBI agent?"

"I'd like to see you, or Walker, do any better."

"You're right, I'd bet you'd like to see anything about now."

"Kirby." The man called Walker ripped off a length of duct tape. Probably meant for her. "This isn't some old Western movie. As you can see, or maybe not, they don't have to knock you out to take you out. Just outsmart you."

Gemma laughed again. "You guys are clueless, though Walker's getting warmer."

"We didn't ask for your two cents, Ms. Saint," Blade said. "A person in your position has no right to be laughing."

"Maybe not. But the IQs of those two boys added together are more than all of ours combined. If you three had any common sense, you might be like Forrest Gump compared to Josh and Caleb."

Walker slapped the length of tape over her mouth.

* * *

Blade sent Walker to pull their van into the garage.

The humming of the garage door closing sounded and, a few seconds later, Walker entered the living room.

"Any sign of the boys?" Blade said.

"No. But Saint's SUV is sitting out there for anyone to see, if they come down the driveway. Should I pull it into the other side of the garage?"

Blade shook his head. "Leave it out there for now, until I decide what we're going to do with Ms. Saint."

It was a strange scene and a strange turn of events that brought Gemma Saint to them. She must have gone solo to try to get the boys. But maybe this was supposed to be some kind of a trap. If so, Blade hadn't figured out what kind of trap, and that bothered him. Regardless, they needed to find those boys.

"I'll get the boys," Blade said. "They're probably lost in the woods. Walker, you stay with Kirby. I don't trust him to watch Saint even if she is tied up."

"How can I watch her? I'm blind.'

"No. You're not blind. We'll get you to an eye doctor as soon as we can." Blade paused. "Quiet for a minute. There's another car coming down the driveway. It will stop when it reaches Saint's SUV."

Blade's phone rang. He swore. "I can't believe this. It's Carr again. Walker, go into the trees and see who's coming. It might be our chopper crew, our returning heroes who bombed an empty boat."

Walker dropped the tape on the floor and grabbed his rifle. "What if it's not them?"

"Then stop them. Hold them off. I'll help as soon as I get rid of Carr."

He picked up the call. "Sikes."

"Blade, there's an investigation into a helicopter attack on a boat. The TV networks are reporting that something looks suspicious. You need to eliminate everyone outside of our team who knows about this operation, especially Gemma Saint and Lex James."

"What about James's twin boys. They're only four, but they're also not your normal preschoolers. Rumor has it their IQs are off the charts."

"Once we have Saint and James, can we really let two kids go free who can identify us?"

"Don't you mean *identify me*?"

"You, me? What does it matter? We all go down. Eliminate everyone who can link the FBI or the DOJ to any of your activities."

"What if it turns out that includes KC Daniels?"

Carr swore until he was short of breath.

A desk job could do that pretty quickly to a bureaucrat like him.

Carr sucked in a deep breath. "How did you let the scope of this get so out of control?"

"Let's get this straight, Carr. It wasn't me who gave Daniels a part in this little drama. It was Lex James. Do you really want the DOJ to be associated with taking out KC Daniels? If you take her out, you know you'll have to take out her husband, Brock, too. He's a baseball star and a national hero. What about their kids? Where does it stop, Carr? When I get killed for doing your dirty work? I think maybe I should disappear and leave you holding the bag."

"You do that and you're dead, Blade."

"Says who? Surely not you. You might have come up through the ranks, but you're nothing but a bureaucrat siting on his fat, numb rump drawing a fat salary and trying to play with American politics ... for a fee. I believe they call that pay to play. Well, I'm just about through playing. Goodbye, Maximillian, I've got bigger problems to deal with right now." Blade ended the call.

"We need to get paid, Blade," Walker said. "You shouldn't push him that far. He *is* the Deputy Director. What if he turns on us?"

"He won't. He's afraid we'll leak information and then disappear. It only takes one little investigation to end Carr's career and maybe give him a nice orange suit."

"Walker, drag Saint into the bedroom and lock her in. Watch out for anyone armed with a squirt gun."

Walker chuckled and scooped up Gemma. He slung her over his shoulder and headed down the hallway.

She tried to knee Walker in the face, but her bound ankles interfered.

Blade turned to Kirby. "You want to handle the James Gang?"

"What do you mean, Blade?"

"How do you feel about those twins?"

"I'd like to wring their scrawny little necks?"

"Okay. After we use them to get Lex James, you get to kill them."

"But—"

"Just do it, Kirby. It might save your worthless hide."

"What about Saint?"

"You're not getting her. I am. She owes me for the trouble she's caused. She'll pay for everything and, when she does. she won't be laughing about Forrest Gump."

Her life would not be like a box of chocolates, because Gemma Saint would know exactly what she was going to get.

Chapter 25

With KC's32 M4 in the floorboard by his feet and the .38 she had given him in his shorts pocket, Lex rode shotgun.

KC drove her SUV down Indian Ford Road about six miles north of Sisters.

They were less than a mile from the driveway to a place that would either fill Lex's heart with joy or the most profound grief Lex had ever experienced.

Before that time, his heart would continue its drum solo, beating out a rhythm that left his mind rattled and his hands shaking.

"Is that the driveway?" KC pointed to a road winding through the pine trees on their right.

"That's it. It's a long driveway and the house is surrounded by pine trees. Not real dense, according to the satellite pictures, but enough for cover, if we don't go closer than seventy-five or a hundred yards."

"You're pretty observant."

"It pays to be observant if you make your living investigating and reporting on government scandals and corruption." He looked across at KC's face.

She appeared calm. No signs of *her* hands shaking.

"Is it always like this before going into a fight, KC?"

"When you don't know how things will go, it's nerve wracking. I understand why some soldiers—uh, soil their clothes." She turned in and stopped. "Let's look through the gaps in the trees to make sure they can't see us yet. And we need to finalize our plan as soon as we can see where things are located."

"Do you think they'll use Josh and Caleb or Gemma as shields?"

"Not if we can surprise them." KC gave him that enigmatic smile that said you have no idea what's going through my mind right now.

And she was right. But it drove Lex crazy, almost as crazy as when Gemma gave him that smile.

But Lex James had several ideas in his head. First, exchange himself for the boys. Second, exchange himself for Gemma. Neither would be possible if they had the boys, because with them, the Fibbies could control Lex James. But what if Lex James wasn't with KC? Maybe he could—

"You're trying to extract Josh and Caleb, aren't you?" KC rolled the SUV slowly forward.

He nodded.

"Let's wait until we get the lay of the land before we do any more planning. There are always surprises when you finally arrive at the battlefield. And with the sun still up, staying hidden will be difficult."

"For what it's worth, now that I've drug you into this, I'm glad I've got an experienced warfighter with me."

"Warfighter? I've been through three or four firefights. That doesn't make me a warfighter. And, Lex, you didn't drag me in. When thugs kidnap little boys from my house, I'm in all the way. I know it's wrong, but right now, I don't really want to save them for the justice system. I just want to take them all out."

"There's my SUV." He pointed ahead, beside a dense stand of pine trees.

"I'm stopping. Let's leave my car here and move on foot to your car. Maybe we can use it for cover while we check out the house."

They both got out and crept through the tree shadows toward Lex's SUV.

"I'd hoped that we'd see Gemma waiting here. But she set herself up to get caught. What she was thinking?"

"Probably the same thing you're thinking about. Those two boys. Something happened in the short time she and boys were together, didn't it?"

"Yeah. The boys thought they'd found their mother and, Gemma didn't say much, but you could see it in her eyes. But, no matter how you slice it, she lied to me in that note, KC."

"To save your life, you numbskull. And the boys' lives too."

He didn't reply.

The pain of reading Gemma's note, KC's rebuttal to it, and now a battle with all their lives on the line—it wasn't a time for arguing with KC.

"Get down. I think I saw the house." KC slunk down near the ground and scurried to the back of Lex's SUV.

Lex followed her.

When they lifted their heads to the missing rear window, Lex was looking through the tinted windshield to see the house. It was unlikely anyone could see them from the house, nearly a hundred yards away.

Gemma's in there.

That thought ate away at him like hydrochloric acid.

Forget her. Gemma lied, dude.

But I think I love her.

You're crazy, man. Don't do anything rash.

He couldn't help it. His thoughts had become a rash of rash thoughts and, in a few seconds, he was going to act on one of them.

"KC, if I could offer myself for Gemma, or the boys, I could get inside. Maybe make something happen."

"You'd make something happen, alright. Two murders … or more."

"Uncalex, they're bad men. Don't go in there."

Lex whirled and then lowered his gun.

Josh and Caleb stood hardly ten feet away.

Lex pulled them behind the SUV then knelt and wrapped his arms around them. "Are you okay?"

"We're okay," Josh said.

"How did you get away?"

"Caleb shot them with his squirt gun."

That didn't make sense, but he had the boys in his arms, two very bright boys. "Josh, Caleb, do you know who's in the house?"

"Yeah. A really bad guy called Blade. Another guy named Walker and Kirby. But Kirby can't see much."

"What about Gemma?"

"Walker snuck up on her and got her while she was 'gotiating with them."

"Is she okay?"

"Uh, I think so," Josh said. "But we haven't seen her since Walker took her inside."

Caleb wiped his eye. "Don't let them hurt her, Uncalex."

Lex looked up at KC. "The odds are better than we thought. I need to go in there." Lex stood and released the boys.

"That's stupid, really stupid, Lex. Once they have you and Gemma, they can kill you both and their mission is complete."

"I've got to try. If this goes badly, will you—"

"It won't go that way if you don't go in."

He turned and faced KC. "But will you make sure that—"

"You know I would." She looked down at the twins then back at Lex.

"You both mind KC until I get back." Lex looked down at the boys.

Josh was gone.

"Caleb, where's Josh?"

Caleb shrugged. "Maybe he had to go to the bathroom."

Lex scanned the area around the vehicles and around the trees behind them.

KC tapped his shoulder and pointed toward the back corner of the garage. "He just came out of the trees, headed toward the garage."

"Caleb, you know where he's going, don't you?"

Caleb hung his head and nodded. "To the garage. There's a doggie door back there."

Lex gripped Caleb's shoulders. "He's not planning to go inside, is he?"

"He won."

"What do you mean?"

"Josh said to pick a number from one to ten. I picked four and he said I lost. But I think he cheated so he could go."

"Caleb, when we get home I'm going to—" The reality was they may not get to any home on planet Earth.

KC laid her hand on Lex's shoulder. "At least they both didn't go."

"It was a dumb thing to do."

"Like what you wanted to do, Lex?"

"For a kid it's dumb."

"I don't think so." Caleb avoided looking at Lex's eyes.

"You don't think so. So why wasn't it a dumb thing to do?"

Finally, Caleb met Lex's gaze with burning intensity in his young eyes and determination painted on his face. "Cuz Josh got two hundred and you don't. You'll see, Uncalex."

* * *

"Kirby, Blade, Walker!"

Blade turned toward the hallway and looked down it. Where had those words come from? It sounded like a kid, one of the twins. "Did you hear that, Walker?"

"It's those boys. We need to grab them before they get away."

"You mean before Lex James finds out we don't have them?" Blade said.

"We still have Gemma Saint," Walker said

"I don't trust Kirby's judgment on her and James's relationship. She may not be enough to hold him off."

The shrill voice sounded again. "We know who you are and what you did. If you don't let Gemma go, we're gonna tell the president."

Blade swore.

"The kid knows how to hit right where it hurts," Kirby said.

"Shut up, Kirby. Nobody's going to get the chance to tell the president anything."

Walker stood. "The garage. Let's get those two nits."

Blade ran down the hallway and flung open the door to the garage.

The rear end of a small boy slipped through the pet door and it closed behind him.

Walker stood in the doorway to the house. "Don't let him get away."

Blade glanced back at him. "I've got the little runt."

Blade ran to the side garage door and pulled it open.

The kid was running toward the trees near the back corner of the house.

Walker looked out the open door. "He's getting away."

"Not going to happen."

Blade sprinted toward the trees where the kid was headed.

Chapter 26

"I thought I heard Josh." Lex crept forward through the trees toward the garage on the right side of the house.

He glanced back when he heard footsteps behind him.

KC followed with her M4 in ready position.

Josh came into view around the corner of the garage. He ran full speed for the trees forty yards ahead.

A large man rounded the corner of the garage. He spotted Josh and took off after him.

Lex stiffened, then lurched forward. He had to get to Josh before the man reached him.

The staccato cracking of an automatic rifle near his right ear stopped him.

Dirt exploded into the air in front of the man.

Josh kept running.

The man whirled and leaped for the protection of the garage.

"Darn!" KC blew out her disgust in a sharp blast. "I wanted to shoot him. Should have shot him, but I ... held back. Killing someone isn't ..."

"It's okay. You saved Josh, KC. But wait till I get my hands on that rascal."

Caleb peeked around KC's side. "Uncalex, you need to ask Josh what he was doin' before ya' do somethin' ya' might regret."

"Maybe you *should* ask," KC placed a hand on Caleb's head.

"Maybe." Lex circled through the trees until he reached Josh.

"Uncalex, I—"

"Listen, Josh," Lex pulled him into the trees and headed back to KC's location. "These men are dangerous. They're killers. Never do that again."

"I told them we knew their names and we're gonna tell the president if they hurt Gemma."

"Great! That's just great."

KC and Caleb stepped out from behind a large tree.

Lex pulled Josh toward them. "Did you hear that, KC?"

"You mean about Josh's threats to the FBI?"

"Yeah. We're all threats because we can identify them, and Josh just confirmed that. Now *all* includes you, KC. If they didn't want all of us before, they do now."

"But they can't be sure who's out here. Especially after hearing automatic rifle fire." KC scanned the house and garage. "It looks like they're all back inside the house. We'd better take advantage of that to come up with a plan to spring Gemma and then get out of here."

"That's okay for starters," Lex said. "But we need more than that. We've got to find someone in the DOJ that we trust, someone who has enough clout to start an investigation to clean house in that whole department, maybe our intelligence organizations too."

KC nodded. "When we can't get justice from the Department of Justice, the whole nation's at risk of either imploding or exploding."

"At least we have one thing going for us."

"You mean president Gramm?"

"Yeah. A person with some integrity. The DOJ is under his administration. Worst case, he can fire our do-nothing Attorney General and bring in a housecleaner," Lex said.

"Only if he can get the senate to approve them. When part of his own DOJ, half of Congress, and much of the judiciary turn on a president, it can *completely stop* an administration." KC pushed the safety lever on her rifle. "Or *completely start* a rebellion."

Lex pointed toward the vehicles. "We can't solve our nation's problems here. Let's work on solving the problem of freeing Gemma. Got any ideas?"

"Uncalex?"

"Not now, Josh. KC and I need to decide how we're going to rescue Gemma."

"But, Uncalex—"

"Josh, I told you—"

Caleb grabbed his arm. "You gonna plan without all the facts?"

"What do you mean?"

"You didn't ask us how we got away or what we found out when we were in that house."

KC mussed Josh's hair. "He's right. We could use a little intelligence."

"Yeah," Caleb said. "We got two hundred and mom always said we should give to people who are less—who don't ..." Caleb's big Brown eyes looked up at Lex, then at KC.

KC covered her mouth with her hand. It looked like she was about to laugh.

Lex got the message. "Poor Uncle Lex with an IQ from the dregs of the genius barrel needs you to give him some intelligence."

"Yeah. I can. There's three bad guys in there, Blade, Walker, and Kirby," Josh said.

"Yeah," Caleb said. "But only two of them can see."

KC lifted Caleb's chin and looked into his eyes. "Do you mean one of them is blind?"

Caleb moved her hand and nodded. "I blinded him. That's how Josh and I excaped'd him."

"Yeah," Josh nodded. "We put toilet bowl cleaner with bleach in Caleb's squirt gun and shot Kirby in the eyes."

"Yeah. And when he yelled, I shot some in his mouth. Then he went crazy and we got away through the doggie door."

Lex put a hand on both twins' heads. "Didn't someone say every generation born is an invasion of civilization by little barbarians, who must be civilized before it's too late? What am I going to do with you two?"

One corner of KC's mouth turned up. "Well, you'd better not underestimate them, like Kirby obviously did. Based on the *intelligence*, we may have only two men to deal with to get Gemma out. Our odds are getting better."

"Except they have the oddsmaker ... Gemma. And I'm afraid of what they might do to her."

"You could tell them the truth, Lex. It couldn't hurt."

"What truth?"

"That you love Gemma." KC's gaze locked on his.

The boys focused on him too.

"Come on, KC. Why would you say something like—"

"Because it's true."

"You don't love someone after only—look, if I said that, they would use her to control me."

"So, are you saying it's true? You're sure not denying it."

"We runned off Melissa, but we'd never do that to Gemma," Josh said.

"Yeah. We'd never get rid of Gemma, 'cause she's like Mama."

Caleb's remark hit Lex in his mental solar plexus, derailing his train of thought and knocking out all his words. The boys were already attached to Gemma, though they had spent only a short time with her. But Gemma had detached herself from Lex. The outcome looked like a lose-lose-lose proposition.

Lex shook his head. "How could telling these thugs something like that possibly help?"

"Think about it, Lex. As long as they have her and not you, they won't hurt her, *if* they're convinced you have some strong feelings for her."

"I already told'em not to hurt her, because she was gonna be our mama, but I'll tell'em again," Josh said.

"You make one move toward that house and I'll lock you in my SUV."

"Uncalex, the sun's not down yet. We'd suffercate," Josh said.

"Yeah. And die of heat exhaust."

"Heat exhaust? You two are full of that."

Josh raised his eyebrows.

Caleb looked at Josh and shrugged.

"Back to Gemma," Lex said.

KC stuck a thumb out at the twins. "Sounds like your boys, with their two hundred, already took care of her for the time being."

He didn't reply. How does a person admit that his four-year-old knows more about relationships than a twentysomething father?

KC studied the house through a tiny gap in the trees. "It would help if we knew where she was in the house."

"Probly where they put Caleb and me."

"Yeah, in the big bedroom on the other side of the house from the garage," Caleb said.

"Well, now we know something," KC said.

Lex nodded. "We do. And that's where I'll break in as soon as it gets dark."

KC stared at him like she was waiting for something.

Lex stared back at her, and his blank stare was all she was going to get.

The whole subject of Gemma was irritating him and, now, he was supposed to tell the Fibbies he loved her?

"Well," KC said. "If that look is all you've got, it's not much of a plan. Only enough to get you killed over a woman you don't give a rip about."

Chapter 27

Blade moved the living room curtain an inch to the side and studied the area in the trees where the shots had come from.

It was still light outside, but he saw no one. "Did you see the shooter?"

"No. But I'm guessing it was a military rifle," Walker said. "AK-47s don't crack like that. And it was *not* a semi-automatic."

"Fully automatic," Blade said. "Where would Lex James get a gun like that? Maybe he has help out there."

"You mean help like those two little monsters that are too smart for their own good?"

"No. Like KC Daniels. With her in on it, they could have recruited some others. Maybe an army."

"Come on. You don't believe all those stories you've heard about her. They're just legends. Hyperbole and myth."

Blade shook his head. "Legends don't shoot at you in automatic mode. I barely made it back to the garage. We don't know how many are out there. We could be outmanned and outgunned."

Blade pulled out his secure phone. "I'm calling Drake and the chopper crew. They can be here by the time it gets dark, and they can come in behind whoever's out there. He can take them out or, at least, tell us how many there are. Right now, our little saint may be the only thing that's keeping them from attacking us."

"Speaking of Ms. Saint," Walker said. "I'm going to the bedroom to check on her. I don't like the way Kirby was looking at her. If he were to do anything to her, and we needed her for a hostage—well, it might not go well."

"Kirby can't even see her, Walker."

"No. But he remembers what she looks like. That's enough to distract any red-blooded male."

Blade chewed on his lip and weighed his options. "Check on him. If you're certain he's becoming a liability ... kill him."

"You sure?"

"Yes. Just like we'll do with Ms. Saint if she loses her usefulness."

Chapter 28

You are an idiot, Gemma Saint.

She had completely alienated Lex and then tried to make a deal with three depraved men to free the twins. But she had gotten captured only to find out the twins had escaped, evidently making a fool out of Kirby in the process, a blind fool.

But Kirby wasn't completely blind, and he had expressed far too much interest in Gemma when they had locked her in the master bedroom with her hands zip-tied and her feet taped together. Then he had tossed her on the king-size bed.

Something was happening outside. The Twins were gone but, sometime after she learned of their escape, there were gunshots.

Gemma had thoroughly discouraged Lex. If he had come, he was probably here only for his boys. If so, he had likely found them by now, so he had no reason to stay. No logical reason. Unless … maybe he couldn't forget those thirty-six hours they had spent together and all that had happened between them.

Their feelings ran too deep to deny. Their needs, each supplied by the other—it all seemed orchestrated by Someone who knew what Lex, Gemma, and the twins needed.

Gemma Saint, you've read too many romance novels.

But didn't someone say the Bible was the greatest romantic suspense story ever written?

Great! Now she was a schizophrenic, having an argument with herself.

She drew a sharp breath when Kirby approached and hovered over her. He squinted and blinked his eyes as if trying to focus on her ... on all of her.

Though he couldn't see clearly, even those attempts brought a sickening sense of defilement. And then, they brought anger.

Gemma pulled her knees to her chest and kicked.

Her feet caught Kirby in the chest and sent him stumbling backward. He crashed into the wall. His breath blasted from his mouth. Now he lay on the floor wheezing like an asthmatic.

She had knocked the breath out of him.

What would he do to her when he recovered? She was too angry to be frightened about it.

The bedroom door flew open.

Walker stood in the doorway. "What's going on in here, Kirby?"

Still trying to suck in a breath, Kirby couldn't reply.

Gemma glared at Walker. "Nobody does that to me. Walker, take off these ties and I'll kill him!"

Cool, self-controlled Gemma had lost it, but she didn't care.

"As much as I would like to see that," Walker pulled something on his rifle and it made a metallic click.

Gemma jumped as three shots left her ears ringing. She sat up on the edge of the bed.

Kirby stopped trying to catch his breath. He was beyond breathing now.

Blood pooled on the hardwood floors near his chest.

Walker had murdered Kirby in front of her.

Gemma had said she wanted to kill Kirby. But after seeing the reality of violent death, she couldn't do that to another human being.

Gemma glared at Walker again. "You murdered him."

"That's not how I interpret it. I—"

Blade appeared in the doorway. "I was afraid of that."

"Look, Blade," Walker said. "I had to—"

"Walker, I agree. Kirby was a liability."

Gemma met Blade's searing glare. She broke eye contact and stared at the floor.

"Ms. Saint, the minute you become a liability—well, you get the picture, I'm sure. So you have a strong incentive to cooperate."

That depends.

The first inkling that her cooperation endangered Lex or the boys and Gemma would attack Walker, Blade, whoever was nearest. And she would not stop her kicking, screaming assault on them until they shot her like they did Kirby. And that would free Lex and the twins.

She looked into Blade's threatening eyes and tried to project her feelings about him and Walker.

Blade cut into Gemma with his searing gaze. "I'm concerned about your attitude, Ms. Saint. You're giving me a real Gemma dilemma."

"She's trouble, boss," Walker said.

"The first time she acts like trouble, you have my permission to be my *trouble shooter.*" Blade's mouth curled into a sneer.

Gemma shouldn't provoke them. She looked at Kirby's body face up on the bedroom floor. Then she looked away from his haunting, lifeless eyes.

"Drag him out of here, Walker."

"Where?"

"To the garage. I'm going back to the living room to watch for our visitors hiding in the trees."

"What about her?"

Blade shot Gemma a piercing glance. "I'm going to lock you in. I would advise you to try living up to your name, Ms. Saint." He shoved her back onto the center of the bed.

Before the door closed, Gemma was already scanning the room for anything that might cut through the ties on her hands or the tape around her ankles.

She rolled off the bed onto the floor and looked under the dresser.

Nothing.

Then under the bed.

Two objects lay about three feet back under the bed. One was short, the other long.

She rolled over and positioned her head to look under the bed.

Caleb's squirt gun and something that looked like a golf club.

Had the boys used these to get away? They'd at least used the squirt gun. Knowing those two, they may have used the gun and the club and hid them on their way out.

Maybe they had saved Gemma Saint's life. At a minimum, they had given her a way to go down fighting.

But first she had to free her hands.

Chapter 29

"KC, those three gunshots from the house ... could they have shot Gemma?" It was the third time he had asked her in the last forty-five minutes, but it was the question driving Lex crazy, threatening to make him do something crazy.

"I don't think they would do that. If they had, they would have immediately made a move to get you before you could get away."

"The sun's been down for a while. It's getting dark here in the trees." Lex looked at KC's shadowy face.

She nodded.

"KC, they haven't tried to come out of the house or tried anything."

"That's right."

"Why?"

"I barely missed the last guy who tried to come out of the house. They're not anxious to face automatic weapon fire."

"Then what are they doing in there?" Lex peered through the trees at the faint light from the house.

"Waiting?"

He turned to face KC. "You think they're waiting for help, don't you?"

"That's why you should have let me take the boys to Benjie's grandparents' house like I suggested over an hour ago."

"But if I can work my way to that bedroom window and free Gemma, the stalemate's over."

"Over? If you try that and make one little slip, it'll be your life that's over. Then they would kill Gemma, because there would be no reason to hesitate. Lex and Gemma dead. Mission accomplished. Is that what you want?"

He didn't reply.

"If they try anything, your boys in the SUV may not be safe. I think we should—"

"Don't move!" A raspy voice came from behind them.

KC froze beside him.

Lex whispered to her. "The boys. I have to take these guys out before—"

"Stop talking and drop your guns. Now!"

KC lowered her rifle to the ground.

Lex jumped when a gun behind him cracked. He flinched when dirt from the bullet stung his bare leg. His gun was in his hand near his stomach, hidden from the men behind. He flipped it toward the trunk of a big pine tree.

The small gun slid into a thick bed of pine needles.

Had they seen it?

"Hands on your head."

Lex complied.

A flashlight beam hit his face. "Well, well, if it isn't the elusive Lex James," raspy voice said.

"Drake ... " A deeper voice came from trees to Lex's right. "Hit Ms. M4 with the light."

The beam moved to KC's head.

"Now, turn around ... really slow."

"It's her, Drake," deep voice said.

"Well who did you expect, Ensley? They've got Gemma Saint inside."

"I didn't expect KC Daniels," Ensley said.

Someone whistled a soft wolf whistle.

"Don't even think about it, Petrelli," Drake said. "She's like your thermobaric grenade. When she goes off, somebody's going to get burned. We'll let Sikes decide what to do with her."

"Would you like to tell us how you and Ms. Saint survived our visit on the lake?"

"Sure. You and your crew are just like your friend, Kirby, the dufus that my four-year-old sons took out."

"What in blazes are you talking about?"

"I'm talking about you."

"Lex, no ..." KC said. "Don't provoke them."

"My son Caleb took out Kirby. You're nothing but a bunch of liars and idiots. Didn't that oath you took mean anything to you?"

"Lex?"

"Keep talking, James," the raspy voice said. "My reasons for keeping you alive until we get to the house are evaporating like water on the Sahara."

KC elbowed him.

"I agree with the sentiment, Ms. Daniels. But keep your distance, or I'll kill you here and let Blade worry about it later. In fact, I think I'll tell him about you now."

Drake slung his gun over his shoulder, pulled out his phone, and placed a call.

"Blade, Drake here. We caught some prowlers ... Yes, we got both of them ... You thought there were more? ... The boys? What boys? ... Okay, we'll look for them, then bring Lex James and KC Daniels in ... Yes, we're sure it's Daniels ... And, Blade, she was carrying an M4 like she knows how to use it ... See you in about five."

Drake ended the call.

Petrelli backed away from the other four and moved closer to the SUV.

Lex looked at KC and pointed one of the thumbs on his head at the SUV where the boys were hidden, then looked at Drake, who was tucking his cell in its holster.

KC dipped her head enough for him to notice. She understood and she was in.

As Lex turned to face Drake, he sought something to provoke the man. He did know the genus and species for the most populous *drake* in the area. "Hey, Mallard."

Drake looked up. "You talking to me, dead man?"

"Yeah. To you, the *anas platyryunchos*."

"What did you just call me?"

Lex slid his right foot back a few inches.

Drake stepped in front of Lex.

Ensley stiffened and raised his rifle.

Lex stepped into his punch and landed it on Drake's nose, splattering blood across the man's face.

KC grabbed the barrel of Ensley's gun with both hands and used her weight to take the barrel to the ground.

Ensley's finger had been on the trigger.

KC's weight pulled down on the gun.

It fired a burst at the ground.

Ensley yelled, at first, unintelligible, then it turned to a vile description of what bullets feel like when they hit a person's toes.

As Drake caught his balance, Lex swung a foot around into the side of the leg Drake had planted.

He hit Drake's knee.

The knee gave.

Drake cried out and crumpled to the ground, holding his knee.

Petrelli jammed the barrel of his gun into KC's head. "Stop! Everybody! Or Daniels is dead."

In about five seconds, they had done more damage than Lex thought possible. But, most importantly, Petrelli had not gone to the SUV to look for the boys.

Lex prayed the twins had heard the conversation and snuck into the woods. But now, he and KC had to face the wrath of two injured men. Lex and KC had put a big hurt on them physically and on their pride. They could expect brutality in return.

Ensley sat on the ground with blood soaking the toe of his left boot.

Drake struggled to his feet, unable to put weight on his left leg.

Petrelli still held his gun to KC's head.

Lex glared at Drake. "Can't blame a guy for trying."

"Yes, I can. You're dead and I'm going to be the one to make that happen ... right after Sikes finishes his enhanced interrogation."

"Drake, we need to get these two inside the house before they force us to kill them. That would make Sikes unhappy. You don't want to see him un—"

"I know, Petrelli." Drake unslung his gun. "Did you check out the SUV for the kids?"

"I took a look inside just before the excitement—"

"You mean before the *stupidity*, Petrelli! The gross stupidity." Drake lifted his left foot off the ground and leaned against a tree, cursing Lex's lineage until Drake ran out of ancestors and words.

Lex glanced down at KC and gave her a brief smile. The boys were safe, for now. Lex's prayer had been answered.

KC dipped her head and then stood after Petrelli goaded her with his gun barrel.

Drake's phone rang. He swore again. "I can't believe this. We're supposed to be the elite of the FBI."

"Hard to believe isn't it?" Lex said in a mocking tone.

KC shook her head at him, her cease and desist signal.

Drake pointed his finger at Lex. "I get you, Mr. James. Do you wanna know how I'm going to do it?"

"Surprise me," Lex said.

"Cut it out, Lex. You've made your point." KC glared at him.

Drake answered the ringing phone, but he must have bumped the speaker button. His call was on the local PA system.

"Drake, what in blazes is going on out there?"

"James and Daniels tried something."

"I heard shots. Are they still alive?"

"Yeah. They're alive, but ..."

"But what? I don't like buts."

Silence.

"Drake?"

"I blew out my knee and Ensley shot off his toes."

"I cannot believe—first you blow up an empty boat, then you let Saint and James get away, and you let a journalist and a woman, unarmed, nearly take all three of you out. Who was it I picked for this *elite* team, the Keystone Cops?"

"Sikes, you can rant all you want, but we've got to get them inside. Ensley's got a puddle of blood under his shoe. He can't walk and neither can I. Can you—"

"I can. I'm sending Walker out now to get you sorry excuses for undercover FBI agents."

"When it's time, I want James all to myself."

"You mean you want a hogtied, completely helpless Lex James."

"Mock me all you want, but I want James. He has a debt to pay."

"As does Gemma Saint to me. We'll see, Drake. Bring in your crew and the prisoners."

"Blade, Ensley can't walk at all. He—"

"He deserved what he got. Either he walks in or I send Walker out to shoot off more than his toes."

Blade ended the call.

Drake looked from the phone to Lex. It was too dark to tell, but the expression on his face said he'd just realized that his entire conversation with Blade went out over the speaker phone.

It's funny what a blown-out knee will make a person forget. Not so funny what it will force them to remember, especially if the memory includes a desire to kill Lex James.

Drake, the person with that desire, glared at Lex with a seething, boiling anger the shadows could not hide.

It sent a tingling sensation up the back of Lex's neck.

Drake had more than a desire to kill Lex. It had become an obsession.

Chapter 30

The moment Marshall Cody Cottrell had discovered the danger to Gemma Saint, he had violated several U.S. Marshal policies, and probably U.S. Code, by having a local member of the FBI's Cyber Task Force, a person Cody trusted, plant a variant of The Finder app on Gemma's phone. Unless she took the batteries out, her cell would be tracked, even if she turned it off.

When Cody snuck out of University Hospital six and a half hours ago, the app had displayed the phone's location as the north end of Crooked River Ranch, Oregon. Cody had zoomed in on the map and learned that the location was the Otter Bench Trailhead.

That raised both questions and concerns. Gemma had not gone on a recreational outing. So was she hiking a trail in a remote area to hide, or was she running for her life?

By the time Cody landed in Redmond, Oregon, forty-five minutes ago, Gemma's phone had moved to a house north of Sisters, Oregon, nearly forty miles from its previous location. How long had it been there? Was Gemma even there?

The sun had long since dropped below the Cascade Mountains to the west. Dusk had begun its transition to darkness as Cody drove his rental car down a small road lined with ponderosa pine trees.

According to the GPS, the house in the woods lay only a couple of miles ahead. Gemma could be in serious trouble. If so, Cody, arriving under cover of darkness, could help her. But what if he were badly outnumbered?

The situation justified calling in outside help, and Cody had a friend who might be able to do just that.

He pulled his rental car off the road at a mailbox turnout and took out his cell. He found Deputy Ramirez in his contact list.

Cody had met Matt Ramirez when they attended the FBI Academy several years ago. The two had hit it off and remained in contact since. But this call, coming out of the blue, may not get the response Cody hoped for.

He placed the call. After five rings it went through to voice mail. Maybe a text would get a better response.

Cody spoke his message into the text box.

Matt, this is Cody Cottrell. Wish this was a friendly chat, but I'm in your neck of the woods and have a problem. Someone outed one of my people in WITSEC. Now rogue FBI agents are trying to kill this person. Can you provide back up? I'm going in cautiously in a few minutes. Once I see what's happening, I'll wait as long as I can for your help. I think this calls for a SWAT team and, with bad cops involved, it could get ugly for anyone involved. Thought you ought to know that before you commit. Here are the GPS coords: 44.370306 -121.58062999999999 It's a vacation house near Sisters. Please pray for me and my charge.

Cody sent the message, put his cell on vibrate, fired a short prayer heavenward, then pulled back onto the road.

The map he had studied showed the house almost a quarter of a mile off the road at the end of a long driveway. That should allow him to park off the road and move through trees to assess the situation.

According to the GPS on his rental car, the driveway was just ahead. Cody spotted the mailbox and then the driveway. He cut his headlights, rolled his window down, turned in, and stopped.

Far ahead, through a gap in the trees, dim lights marked the location of the house.

He pulled off the driveway and rolled across the relatively flat terrain until trees hid his car.

Cody got out and worked his way toward the house by moving parallel to the driveway. After going about two-hundred yards, he spotted two SUVs blocking the driveway.

A hundred yards beyond the vehicles, the lights of the house became visible through the trees. The curtains were drawn. Nothing visible inside the house.

Cody crept to the SUV nearest the house.

"Mister?" A child's voice came from a cluster of trees near the SUV.

Cody froze and waited.

"Whose side are you on?" The child's voice again.

If someone had a gun on him, he probably would have been shot by now. He needed an answer for the child. "I'm on the side of the law."

"From what we saw, that's not a good side."

"Yeah. The FBI is bad, and they don't tell the truth." A second child's voice, almost identical to the first.

Cody was approaching a location where an FBI black operation was possibly being conducted and yet talking to two kids. When he tried to make sense of that, it didn't compute.

He needed to keep the conversation going and, hopefully, gain some useful intelligence. "I know the FBI people here are not good. But I'm not in the FBI. I'm a U.S. Marshall."

"You mean like the marshal who was supposed to protect Gemma?"

"Yes." How did they know about Gemma? What else did they know about her?

"Then you aren't too good either. Uncalex and KC had to do your job for you."

This discussion was going downhill fast. "You're right. But I got shot. I'm here now."

172

"He's lyin', Josh. He don't have no bandages or anything and he wasn't limping."

"That's because I got shot in the head."

"That's the biggest whopper you told us yet," the unnamed boy said.

"Yeah. You'd be dead if they shot you in the head," Josh said.

"I almost was. I went to a hospital."

"What's your name?"

"Cody Cottrell."

"That's him, Cabe. The marshal Gemma told us about."

"Unless he's lyin' again."

Joshua and Cabe, probably Caleb. Twin boys, and they had spent time with Gemma. What else did they know? "Who's in the house, boys?"

"It's alright to tell him that, Josh. We'll see how he re-axes."

"There are six FBI men in there. One of them is blind."

"Yeah. And they have Gemma, Uncalex, and KC."

"KC? Do you mean KC Daniels?"

"Yeah. She's our aunt ... well, sorta'. We call her Aunt KC. Mister, we were in that house. They captured us. If you want to know what's inside, where everything is, we can tell you."

"You mean that you two got away from the FBI?"

"Only one was watchin' us. We blinded him with a squirt gun and got away."

"Now who's telling whoppers?"

"Honest, mister. It's true."

"Yeah. We squirted bleach in his eye."

Bleach in his eye? Again, it didn't compute.

The two boys stepped out from behind the trees. They looked about four. Too young to be having this discussion and too young to be in this place of danger.

It was best for Cody to ignore the anomalies and go for more information. "Where do you think they have Gemma?"

"She's probly tied up in the bedroom. That's where we were."

"But maybe she's with them in the living room. Oh, the FBI's car is in the garage."

"How long ago did they take Lex and your aunt to the house?"

"Just a minute ago," the twin on the left said.

"Thanks. You guys are a great source of intelligence."

"Yeah. About two hundred."

Two hundred what? He hoped it wasn't two hundred whoppers. "Okay. Well, you two stay back here behind the cars. There might be some shooting. Whatever you do, don't approach the house."

Neither replied.

Not a good sign, especially coming from these two who acted and thought like someone three or four times their age. "I mean what I said. Always keep the car and a lot of trees between you and the house."

"We already had bullets shot at us, mister. We're not stupid."

"Josh, we don't know who shot those bullets."

"I can see that you understand," Cody said. "I'm going in now and try to find that bedroom."

As Cody crept through the trees toward the house, he saw no signs of life, no shadows on the curtains.

Was the FBI team waiting for him to approach? It didn't matter. He was Gemma Saint's inspector. She was his charge. And he would give his life to save her. He almost had.

Chapter 31

Gemma lay on the bathroom floor, on her back, when the gunshots sounded. A single burst, then the cry of people in pain.

She had prayed it wasn't Lex. It hadn't sounded like his voice, but she'd never heard him in physical pain.

Now, fifteen minutes later, she worked on freeing her hands. But that started with freeing her feet.

Gemma's ankles, bound with two layers of duct tape, slid back and forth on the sharp edge of the bathroom counter.

She lifted her head from the floor and studied the frayed edge of the tape. Progress. Painfully slow, but progress.

She arched her back and pushed up with her hands to place more weight on the tape.

The tape tore half-way through. Probably the cheap imitation tape from China.

Gemma raised her legs and dropped them hard onto the corner of the counter.

The tape ripped all the way through.

She set her feet on the floor and pulled one ankle at a time from the sticky wrapper of tape still clinging to her skin. That skin had turned raw and red. Blood appeared on her right ankle.

She rolled onto her stomach and rocked back onto her knees. Finally, Gemma rose to her feet.

By backing up to the counter, she worked the zip tie on her wrists into position on the edge of the counter.

The counter edge had cut into duct tape, but could it do the same with the plastic tie?

Gemma started the awkward contortions required to saw back and forth on the counter edge.

Within a minute, her wrists stung where the skin had been worn away. Within two minutes, the sticky warmth of blood lubricated the ties and her wrists. The stinging radiated down into her hands and up her arms.

To keep her mind off the pain, she prayed. First for Lex and KC. Then the boys. Finally, for herself, that no one would come in to check on her until she was free.

* * *

A prod from what felt like a gun barrel sent a stabbing pain through Lex's back as Petrelli forced Lex to walk through the front door.

Where were the boys? They had gotten away, but what were they up to? Probably trying something that could put them in danger.

He shot off a short prayer for the boys, then for Gemma, and KC, and then stepped into the living room.

Behind Lex, Drake's raspy, strained voice cursed KC, trying to make her hurry.

The vile description Drake gave KC almost forced Lex to turn and lay Drake out on the ground with a quick punch. But the damage he and KC had already done had earned them physical abuse that would go far beyond verbal vilification. That's what Lex needed to steel himself for ... pain.

From farther behind Lex, a rhythmic clomping sound came, occasionally split apart by a guttural groan from Ensley, who hopped on one foot and drug the other.

KC was sharp, intuitive, and cool under pressure. A lot like Gemma, but more experienced in what they were facing here, something like a combat situation.

And Gemma—had they hurt her or just held her captive? If at all possible, he needed to see her, to know. But if he asked or demanded, he'd never get to see her.

Blade and Drake were too cruel and arrogant to give in to a prisoner, unless they had no alternative.

Lex studied the men in the room as Petrelli goaded him across it and forced him to stand against a wall with his hands behind him.

Once bound, his fate would be determined, barring some kind of divine intervention. He'd already asked for that a dozen times. But it seemed that it was now or never for granting that request.

As the man called Walker picked up a roll of duct tape, the realization came that Lex had asked for help, but not acted on his request, except when he helped the boys escape.

So why not act now?

Had the question come *from* his mind or *to* his mind.

Someone shoved KC beside him.

Lex met her gaze and nodded.

KC dipped her head. She understood their situation and was ready.

Walker had stopped behind Lex.

He had to strike now.

He whirled and shoved a fist into Walker's throat.

Walker coughed and choked.

KC already had both hands on Petrelli's gun barrel. She kneed him in a vulnerable spot but couldn't pull the gun away.

"Stop, or you're both dead!" Blade's voice.

Lex didn't stop. He shoved the coughing, choking Walker into Blade, spoiling his aim.

Blade's rifle fired once.

A sharp, stinging pain shot through Lex's right triceps.

He couldn't stop now, Petrelli was overpowering KC.

Lex kicked Blade in the groin and reached for his gun, snagging it with his left hand.'

Walker had slumped to the floor choking on his injured larynx.

Ensley watched the fray, holding a bloody cloth over his foot with one hand, the other hand on his rifle, but no sign yet that he would join in.

Blade fought through the pain Lex had given him and tried to work the gun in position to shoot Lex again.

He couldn't let that happen.

And he couldn't help KC.

His wounded right arm still worked and had strength, but blood ran down it to his wrist.

At some point, Ensley might decide to shoot Lex. If he did, the fight would be over in seconds.

If Blade ripped his rifle from Lex's hand, same result.

KC, as game as she was, could never overpower Petrelli. How had she held onto his gun this long?

Lex sucked in a deep breath, roared out his rage, and assaulted Blade with everything he had left. Beating the man, kicking him, glaring into his eyes.

As Blade retreated from the furious assault, for the first time, Lex saw something that gave him a measure of hope, fear in Blade's eyes.

Chapter 32

A commotion somewhere in the house.

Gemma stopped sawing on her zip ties and listened.

Noise came from down the hall in the direction of the living room.

Yelling. Cursing.

A rifle shot cracked.

It sounded like a war. But who was doing what to whom?

With her heart drumming out her panic, Gemma spread her wrists apart, stretching the nylon bands and dropped all her one-hundred-twenty-five pounds on the corner of the counter.

With a sharp sting and a snap, the tie broke.

Gemma scurried to the bed and pulled out her only two weapons, the blue-colored squirt gun and a golf club. The club head was thick and heavy. She spun it around and examined the underside of the head. SW, a sand wedge. The perfect club for pounding a little white ball out of a bunker or pounding someone's bone until it broke.

She positioned her body beside the door where she could reach whatever came through first ... and waited.

* * *

Lex gripped Blade's rifle with both hands.

Blade backpedaled.

Lex stepped in close and head-butted Blade.

Petrelli ripped his gun from KC's hands.

She fell to the floor.

He jammed the gun against her head. "Stop! Everybody! Or she gets it."

Lex pushed off from Blade and stepped back. "We're stopping."

Blade advanced and raised the butt of his rifle to ram it into Lex's face.

"Blade, you stop too!"

The look Blade gave Petrelli was enough to make Lex wince.

But dissension in the ranks—that was a good thing. Maybe something Lex could cultivate.

Lex glanced at KC on the floor. She didn't have any apparent wounds, only a gun pointed at the side of her head.

They would be reluctant to shoot someone as well-known and beloved by Americans as KC, but Lex would give them no provocation when a little pressure on Petrelli's trigger could end KC's life.

Walker could suck in a breath now. But each time he sounded like an asthmatic. And he kept massaging his throat and trying to swallow.

A blow to the Adam's apple could cause a hysterical reaction that was uncomfortable. It could also cause death.

Maybe Lex should have put more power into his punch to Walkers larynx. If Walker's incapacitation had lasted a bit longer, he and KC could have gone another round with Blade and Petrelli.

No. The result would be the same.

Blade backed Lex against the wall. "Now, turn around. Hands behind your back."

Lex responded slowly, trying to come up with a plan of attack that had a chance of success, because once the tape went around his wrists, it was all over ... except for the torture and the dying.

"Put them behind your back, James. If you make one false move, Petrelli will add two new holes to Ms. Daniels' beautiful head. That would be such a shame."

Walker wrapped the tape around Lex's wrists, twice.

They repeated the procedure with KC.

It was done. Interrogation and torture, then death. They had both Lex and Gemma. How long would they wait?

Lex prayed the boys could find a way to get help from a house down the road, from someone, anyone.

He looked at KC.

She didn't look frightened, only sad.

"Walker." Blade pointed down the hall. "Go check on Ms. Saint, then we'll set up our interrogation room in the kitchen where there are some interesting appliances, knives and other pain-producing paraphernalia."

Walker swallowed hard, then smirked as he passed Lex and sauntered down the hallway toward the master bedroom.

Lex wanted to move, look down the hallway, anything to know Gemma was okay.

"You see," Blade said. "It doesn't pay for amateurs to play around with professionals."

"Like them?" Lex nodded toward Ensley, then toward Drake, who had skipped the fight due to his blown knee. "And, of course, the ultimate professional, Kirby. Taken out by two four-year-old kids."

"Carr's not going to like this. Too messy," Petrelli said.

Blade cursed. "Petrelli, loose lips kill people. I believe yours just killed Ms. Daniels."

So Max Carr was calling the shots from 935 Pennsylvania Avenue. Given the man's political bent and ambitions, Lex wasn't surprised. But he needed to stay alive or the story might never make it outside of this room. And it had become obvious that KC's name and reputation would not save her. Carr would tell Blade to kill her and probably the boys too.

* * *

Footsteps in the hallway grew louder.

The fight had ended. Who won? Who was still alive? Who was dead? Gemma prayed it wasn't Lex.

She raised her hands when the doorknob wiggled. Gemma glanced at the sand wedge leaning against the dresser beside her and put her index finger on the trigger of Caleb's squirt gun.

The door swung open.

Walker stuck his head in and never had the chance to see what was coming.

The small soaker gun filled both of his eyes with toilet bowl cleaner.

Walker fell to his knees, hands over his eyes, cursing and screaming.

Gemma grabbed the sand wedge, stepped back and hit the ball, Walker's head, out of the bunker with a single, well-placed stroke.

The screaming and cursing ended. Walker lay, out cold in the doorway.

Footsteps came from the living room.

She scooped up Walker's legs and pulled him into the room, then closed and locked the inside of the door.

Walker lay unconscious at her feet, but he had no weapon on him.

She checked him for a shoulder holster and a hand gun but saw none.

The door lock clicked.

Someone twisted the handle, but the inside was locked.

It would be only a few seconds before whoever stood outside kicked in the door.

Gemma jumped when, behind her, the bedroom window shattered.

A hand gun flew in through the window and landed on the floor near her.

"Uncalex's gun, Gemma. It's got bullets in it."

She grabbed the gun. "Josh, Caleb, hide. Don't let the Fibbies see you."

Gemma leaped to her position beside the door and raised the gun head-high.

The door flew off its hinges and crashed to the floor.

The tip of a gun barrel appeared, then a head.

Gemma pulled the trigger.

The man dropped to the floor. His assault rifle landed in the hallway.

If he was still alive, she was in trouble. This was not the time for taking any chances, taking anything for granted. She was fighting evil, and it was a time to fight to win.

But she could not bring herself to shoot the man lying motionless in the hallway.

Inside the bedroom, Walker moved, then roared in pain, and crawled toward the bathroom.

What if he rinsed his eyes, could see, and came after her? She must stop him, but Gemma couldn't kill him while he was helpless.

She pushed the gun barrel against his shoulder socket and pulled the trigger.

Walker yelled and collapsed on the floor.

Shadows danced in the hallway. Someone was coming from the living room.

After hearing shooting, they would be cautious.

Her gun looked like a .38 caliber revolver. Were they six shooters or five shooters? Best to assume five.

If so, Gemma had two shots left. And the person coming, probably Blade, wouldn't make himself an easy target.

But would he take the chance of hitting one of his own men by accident?

A long burst of gunfire chewed on the door frame and splintered the dresser inside.

Evidently, Blade didn't give a rip about his men.

Gemma backed away from the door, looking for cover.

A gun barrel poked in and fired a short burst.

She shot through the doorway, blowing a hole in the hallway wall. Maybe that would slow the man down. But with only one shot left in her handgun, this would not end well.

Gemma had dropped the sand wedge in the middle of the room after hitting Walker.

She reached for it.

Another burst chewed up the hardwood floor near the club.

She made one more attempt and snagged the sand wedge, then moved to the left of the doorway, praying the man outside did not shoot through the wall where she stood.

A big man leaped into the room firing. He swung the barrel of his gun in an arc. Not knowing her position, he had started his shooting arc on the other side of the room.

She had maybe a second. Gemma swung the sand wedge like a baseball bat into the man's face.

He grunted, stepped back and nearly fell.

She raised her gun and fired.

The gun clicked.

It hadn't been fully loaded.

She raised the sand wedge to hit him again. But she was out of time.

Now, the action seemed to slow. Gemma saw every detail—Blade's rifle swinging her way, the club in her hands accelerating toward his head.

The outcome became clear. Blade's rifle shots would reach her body before her club hit him.

Another rifle fired a long burst, striking Blade in the head and chest.

Blade stumbled backward. He went down hard and didn't move.

"Don't shoot, Gemma."

That voice ... it couldn't be.

A head poked in through the shattered bedroom window.

Cody Cottrell!

"Cody, I thought—"

"Quick, tell me who's where in the house." He slid open the window to avoid the broken glass in the window frame and climbed through.

Gemma tried to organize her thoughts. She tried to answer whatever he had asked, but a muddle of surprise and confusion stopped her.

"Gemma," he pulled her to the far-left side of the room, away from the doorway. "How many FBI are left. I see three bodies here."

That would mean three minus Kirby were left. "There are two. Probably in the living room. One of them is probably wounded. I think they're holding Lex and KC Daniels. I hope they're still alive."

"KC Daniels? How did—"

"Don't ask. Long story."

"Weapons?"

"They have automatic rifles, like that one." She pointed at Blade's rifle in the doorway.

"Can you shoot one?"

"Show me how and I can."

"Could you shoot a person if you had to?"

"I just shot two of them." She pointed at one of the men on the floor.

He nodded and snatched Blade's rifle from the doorway. Then Cody pulled a full magazine from one of the men's pocket and loaded the rifle.

"Here's the safety—on and off. Here's automatic mode. Leave it there."

"Blade, did you shoot Saint?" The voice came down the hall from the living room.

"We need to hurry, Gemma, or we lose all chance of surprising them."

"You okay, Blade?" The same voice.

Cody laid a hand on her shoulder. "We both step into the hallway, you on the left. On my signal, shoot a burst into the ceiling of the living room or high on the wall. Keep your gunfire to the left. I'll be moving toward them on the right side. The gun barrel will try to rise while it fires. Just hold it down as best you can."

"Here's the way it is, Ms. Saint. If you try anything, KC Daniels gets her head shot, immediately." The voice sounded angry but uncertain, maybe frightened.

"So much for surprise. But they think I took out three of their men. They're crazy."

"No, Gemma. You're much stronger than you think." He pointed at the men on the floor. "And I'm banking on there being more strength where that came from. Now, let's go."

"But they said they'd shoot KC. And Lex is in there too."

"We can't give in to their threats and intimidation. When you shoot, their first reaction will be to protect themselves. My job is to not let them have a second reaction."

Gemma nodded, and Cody pulled her into the hallway.

"In the living room ... on which side are the couch and chairs, the places they would sit?"

"The right side."

"Where do you think Lex James and KC Daniels are?"

"Against the wall on the left side."

"Then that's how we'll play it. Let's go."

Cody pressed his body against the right wall and slunk toward the living room.

Gemma pulled the gun into her shoulder, aimed it high to the left, and squeezed the trigger.

The gun came alive in her hands, cracking out a rapid staccato rhythm that both frightened her and sent her on a power trip.

The gun barrel climbed until she blew off part of the hallway ceiling.

Gemma pulled the barrel down slightly and continued firing.

The far wall of the living room took a beating. Pieces of pictures and decorations flew through the air.

Gemma ran out of bullets.

Cody rounded the corner, gun ready, and fired two short bursts.

The house went silent, except for the ringing in her ears.

"Put your gun on safety and come in, Gemma." Cody's voice. "We have control of the house."

Gemma started to run, then slowed and approached the living room cautiously. What would she see there? Lex shot? Something worse?

When she entered the room, Gemma scanned a quick one eighty. The scan stopped on Lex.

What would he think when he saw her? So much had happened that affected their relationship—all her fault or her choice.

Lex sat on the floor, beside KC, both with their hands bound behind them.

He saw Gemma.

Their gazes locked.

Lex smiled.

It was a good sign, an invitation to resume building the deep relationship both had already acknowledged.

Gemma slid onto her knees beside Lex and kissed him. She kissed him again.

"Gemma, at least cut this tape off my hands so I can defend myself."

She looked at KC. "Are you both okay?"

KC grinned. "I would be if someone would get a knife from the kitchen and cut this tape off my wrists."

"Be right back."

"These two won't be giving us any more trouble. They're both dead," Cody said.

"And who might you be? The lone ranger?" Lex frowned and studied Cody.

"No. The lone marshal. Cody Cottrell."

"The dead marshal?"

"The almost dead marshal. They bounced a bullet off my skull. I woke up in a hospital, worrying about Gemma."

"You know, that can be an exercise in frustration. She's unpredictable."

Gemma had heard enough to know there were some major wrinkles to be ironed out between her and Lex. That would have to wait. She hurried to the kitchen to get a knife.

When she returned she went to KC. "Ladies first."

She sawed carefully through the tape until she could rip it off.

KC pulled the tape from her hands and hugged Gemma. "Go easy on Lex." She mouthed the words, "The note."

So the note had hurt him, just as she planned. It was so stupid in hindsight. But he couldn't believe it now, could he?

Gemma slid close to Lex.

He pushed his wrists away from his back, exposing the tape.

"Lex, I didn't know if I'd ever see you again and—oh, the boys."

Lex's eyes focused on the big living room window. "Do you know where they are?"

"I know where they *were*. Josh tossed your pistol to me through the bedroom window. That's how I got two of their men. But I need to back up to tell you—"

"No. You need to cut this tape off me."

She looked across the room at Cody. He was collecting all the weapons.

"Cody, I think Walker is alive. He's in the bedroom. Be careful. He still has the use of his legs and one arm."

Cody stood and strode toward the hallway.

Lex's forehead wrinkled. "Legs and one arm? What did you do to him, Gemma?"

"Caleb's squirt gun was under the bed where they put me. It laid beside a sand wedge. Kirby got both, the squirt gun to the eyes and a sand wedge to the head. After Josh threw in the gun, I shot him in the shoulder for good measure."

"Remind me never to get on the wrong side of Gemma Saint."

KC laughed. "Having to hurt people isn't funny, but taking out half of an elite team of undercover FBI with a squirt gun and a sand wedge—Brock's not going to believe this story."

Gemma studied Lex's eyes wondering when a certain subject would surface. "The boys saved us, along with Cody."

"And you, Gemma." Lex's long steady gaze into her eyes brought the truth home. She, Lex and the boys had survived against insurmountable odds. Something only a good God could accomplish when He erased Gemma's jinx. Maybe it had never really existed, except in her mind.

"Please, Gemma. This tape is killing my wrists."

"Sorry." She reached behind Lex and sawed on the tape.

"Walker's alive." Cody's voice came down the hallway. "But he can't move much, and I think he's nearly blind."

When Lex's hands came free, he reached for Gemma's shoulders. Dried blood painted a dark red trail down his arm.

"You're bleeding. What happ—you've been shot, Lex."

"It's only a deep scratch. I'm fine. Let's go find Josh and Caleb. Then you and I have something to discuss."

KC raised her eyebrows. "Something like ... a little love note left in my bathroom."

Chapter 33

Gemma could never repay the people in this room.

Lex tried to pull her to the living room door, but she stopped him.

Lex, KC, Cody, even the twins had all risked their lives for her. What had been elation turned to a fountain of tears. She couldn't turn it off.

"Are you okay, Gemma?" Lex pulled her head against his chest.

He had done it as if it were the natural thing for Lex James to do. "You had to do some difficult things, Gemma. It's only natural to feel—"

"No. that's not—" Her voice broke and for the next minute she finished soaking the front of Lex's shirt.

"What is it then? As soon as we find the boys, everything will—"

"Police! Everyone in the house, put down your weapons and come out with your hands on your head." The voice blasted from a bull horn, loud and full of authority.

Lights lit the area around the house like a football field on Friday night.

"There's more of them, Lex. Law enforcement that we can't trust. I should have known."

Lex released his hold on her and turned toward Cody.

Gemma looked up and saw Cody smiling. "Do you know who's out there, Cody?"

"Someone I sent a message to before I drove down the driveway to this house. He brought a SWAT team with him."

KC walked to Cody's pile of guns and reached for her M4. "If it's law enforcement, can we really trust them? We'd better be sure before we walk out of this house."

Cody cracked the front door. "Ramirez, is that you?"

"It's me. Quantico?"

"Six years ago."

"No. Nine," the voice on the bullhorn replied.

"We're safe," Cody said. He cupped a hand around his mouth. "We've secured the house. The rogue FBI are all dead except for one badly wounded man. But we'll put down our weapons, even the squirt gun, and come out hands on heads."

"Come on, Cody? Squirt gun? The word's out that you had a bullet bounce off your head and then you snuck out of a hospital. How much damage did that bullet do?"

"We're coming, Ramirez. I'll explain once we're outside."

"The boys—they're still out there." Lex's voice crescendoed. "What if one of the SWAT team spots them and starts shooting?"

"Ramirez, there are four-year-old, identical twins outside. Lex James's boys. Tell your men to be—"

"We've got the little runts. Don't worry about them. But does anybody in there have Triple A?"

Lex's body relaxed. "Triple A? That's a bit off topic."

Gemma draped her arm around his waist. "They're safe, Lex. That's all that matters."

"Cody ..." Lex stepped toward the door and pulled Gemma with him. "I've got to see my boys. I'm going out."

Cody hooked Lex's arm. "Just a second ... Ramirez, we're coming out. There will be four of us. The wounded guy is incapacitated in the master bedroom."

Lex led Gemma out the door into the blinding floodlights.

Gemma tried to shield her eyes with an elbow as she walked with her hands on her head toward four men standing in front of the first tier of trees.

Cody's voice came from behind Gemma. "We're all out."

They walked across the lawn and another twenty yards to the men.

Two members of the SWAT team each held a squirming child with an arm cinched tightly around the kid's waist.

"Put me down. You're nothin' but a bad FBI man. Gemma called you a Fibbie. That's 'cause—"

"Cool it, kid."

A muscular Hispanic man knocked Cody's hands from his head and gave him a manly hug. "Dude, it's sure good to see you come out of there with no holes in you. But I've got a question for you."

"Shoot," Cody said.

"Who or what is an uncalex?"

"That would be me, sir. Lex James."

"Uncle Lex … I get it, and I recognize you now," Ramirez said. "These your boys?"

"That depends. What did they do?"

"They let all the air out of our tires. Both vans."

"Hence the Triple A request," Lex said.

"And it was real hard, Uncalex. But we didn't want the Fibbies to get away before you and KC could shoot'em."

"Yeah," Caleb said. "But we found two of these and it was real easy after that." Caleb held up a bullet with a pointed head.

"Looks like the bullets I dropped when your *Fibbies* got the drop on Lex and me," KC said.

"Put the boys down guys. Who'd have believed two little squirts could strand us out here using two M4 bullets without the gun to go with them."

Lex chuckled. "You'd be surprised what two squirts can do."

KC broke into hysterical laughter.

Ramirez stared at her, hands on his hips. "Well, I don't think it's so funny. I have to explain to my superiors that we had to call a tow truck because two four-year-old vandals flattened our tires."

"Officer Ramirez," Gemma said. "I've got Triple A. Well, I had it with my first fake ID for WITSEC, but with the fake ID I got in Bend, at the college, I guess I don't have it anymore."

"You keep going, Ms. Saint, is it? And I'll have to read you your rights."

"Yes, sir. We wouldn't want that."

Ramirez shook his head. "I'm not sure I want any of this, the expense report or the other reports I have to write up." He gave the order for his men to secure the crime scene, check on the wounded man, and call for an ambulance.

"I've got an idea," Cody said. "While I give your team a guided tour of the crime scene, I'm going to borrow the team leader's secure phone. There's got to be a senior FBI or DOJ person managing this black operation. When the leader, Blade, doesn't check in, the person in charge will call. I want to know who it is. With a little help from a hacker I know, maybe we can follow this conspiracy up the chain of command."

"Good idea, providing you don't create some unusable evidence," Ramirez said.

"As long as I know the person's identity, I can find a lot more evidence."

"Cody, I know that person's identity," Lex said.

"Do you *suspect*, or do you know?" Cody asked.

"He knows." KC said. "We both overheard Blade's conversation with his, uh, boss."

"Well ..." Cody looked from KC to Lex.

"It's Max Carr, the swamp man."

"Then it's still a good idea," Cody said. "Even if the evidence is not directly admissible in a court of law."

Cody took several members of the SWAT team for their tour of the house.

Ramirez walked to Lex's SUV.

Lex and Gemma stood beside the vehicle, each with a boy under their arm.

KC leaned against the front fender.

Ramirez' hands went back to his hips. "Now, does someone want to tell me about that deadly weapon Cody mentioned?"

"Which one would that be?" KC asked, with a smirk on her face.

"The squirt gun."

Lex looked at KC.

She shook her head. "You tell him. Lex."

He blew out a sigh. "This is a story about how two four-year-old geniuses and a beautiful young woman took out an elite FBI team with a squirt gun."

"And a sand wedge, Lex," Gemma said.

* * *

As Gemma listened to Lex tell the story she had played a role in, one word came to mind, incredible.

When overconfident people's arrogance causes them to underestimate others, incredible things can happen. But what happens when people are misjudged in other ways, considered to be untrustworthy liars? What if they had a good reason to lie? Or thought they did?

KC, in a rare moment they had alone, had told Gemma what Lex said after reading the note. "Gemma, Melissa—they're all the same."

For Lex, a man with trust issues, Gemma may have pushed him beyond his point of no return. She was about to find out.

Lex took Josh and Caleb by the hand and handed them off to KC.

She nodded, mouthed something to Lex, and walked off with the boys. She took them away from the house toward the two vans with flat tires parked a short distance down the driveway.

Lex glanced down at his watch. "What a day. It's nearly midnight and it looks like we survived it."

"*We* survived? Did we, Lex?"

He didn't reply, but even in the dim light his face said he understood her question.

Still no reply.

If he wasn't going to say anything, she was.

"You know, people make mistakes, errors in judgement, especially when the stakes are high and when—"

"When they should be going to the people they trust for help, rather than going it alone?"

Gemma's gaze dropped to the pine needles covering the ground. "Yes."

"Do you know what that says about a person's level of commitment to those they supposedly trust?"

Lex had struck a live emotional nerve, more painful than a nerve hit by a dentist's drill.

"All the feelings mean nothing until commitment validates them. Isn't that what you said that day we were hiding by the river? And I haven't demonstrated enough commitment. You think I'm just like Melissa. Maybe if Blade had killed me, you would have seen enough commitment." Tears started flowing before Lex replied, because she knew what was coming.

"After all that happened to us and between us, how could you write that note and say those things—that you were never meant to be a wife or a mother. You know how the boys feel about you."

Gemma wiped her cheeks. "The boys aren't the problem. It's what you feel, or don't, that's the problem."

"But I need you, Gemma."

"You need me for your story, for exposing the corruption. I'm just part of your agenda."

"The boys need you too."

"Lex, if we work together through the entire story, the whole conspiracy against President Gramm, Marsh McDowell's retrial, and the congressional hearings where we will have to testify, we will be together for months. You can't ask me to let those two boys further into my heart only to have you rip them away again."

Lex opened his mouth to speak—

"I'm not finished. How can I do that, with the boys, and with you, with no commitment. I was going to give my life for you and the boys. Lex, you're the one with commitment issues and you can't even see that."

His shoulders slumped. He broke eye contact.

She had never seen Lex look so defeated. Should she have been so—yes. Lex needed to hear the truth about himself.

And about me.

* * *

Dude, what in heaven's name do you think you're doing?

It wasn't in heaven's name. It was in Lex James' name. And, after hearing Gemma slice and dice it, he wasn't proud of it.

How could he put Gemma Saint in the same category as a self-absorbed woman like Melissa? Yes, Gemma had lied to him ... to save Josh's and Caleb's lives. She had gone to die for the boys in a desperate attempt to prevent him from doing the same thing.

He couldn't ask anything more from her. She'd proved her love, devotion, commitment—anything a person could prove about love and caring. And the joy on her face when she found him safe in the living room—he had turned it all to tears.

Lex looked at Gemma leaning against a pine tree, head down, arms folded, crying softly.

He approached her while his heart tried its best to rip his chest apart. Lex James had never been in this kind of situation before and apologies were not his strong suit.

"What do you want?" She didn't look up. But what did he expect?

"A peace offering?"

"Maybe I don't want peace. How about nuclear war?"

Not good. "A love offering, then?"

Gemma sniffed and wiped her nose. "I'm listening."

"I'm a fool."

"You got that right. Maybe I should call you Mel."

Ouch. The masculine form of Melissa. Gemma had a point. A sharp point. And, in his estimation, it had penetrated right where she had wanted it to.

"Could you ever love a fool, Gemma?"

"Aren't you forgetting something?" Her eyes now bored into him. Gemma was looking for something, and her searing gaze burned away everything else.

The question was, would there be anything left when she was done?

But he had forgotten something. "Gemma, could you ever forgive a fool like me?"

"That depends."

"On?"

"Give me a reason, Lex."

"I need you."

"You already told me that." She swiped at her cheeks. "So what's new in your part of the world?" She turned her head away.

"Something that's been growing for about three days now."

"Suspicion? Doubts?"

"Doggone it, Gemma, I love you. I need you. And I want you."

His words brought her head around to face him. The flood lights from the house lit her face. Gemma's eyes had softened. Everything about Gemma had softened.

"What do you really want, Lex James? You'd better ask while I'm still in a listening mood." The corner of her mouth twitched like she wanted to smile ... or was about to cry.

"Please forgive me, Gemma."

"I'll consider it."

"The note hurt, but I should never have mentioned you and Melissa in the same sentence. The same paragraph. The same story. The same—"

"Make that the same universe and I might go for it." A smile tweaked one side of her mouth, then disappeared. "Are you through, Lex?"

"No, I'm just starting. Gemma, would you consider—"

Ramirez and Cody had left the house and strode toward Lex and Gemma. Their timing stunk.

KC put out a hand, giving them the universal stop signal.

The twins used the opportunity to break free. They made a bee line for Gemma.

"I—I need a partner, Gemma."

Where had those words come from?

Dude, you really are an idiot.

"We all need somebody, Lex ... someone who knows our mistakes and loves us anyway."

Who was she talking about, herself or him?

Josh got to Gemma first. He grabbed one hand.

Caleb latched onto the other.

Josh opened his mouth first. Shock and awe time. "We want you to stay and be our mama. We don't want nobody else."

"Yeah," Caleb said. "If you don't stay and watch us, who knows what we might do. We might get captured by the Fibbies again and get shot or somethin'."

Gemma brushed a tear from her cheek and looked at Lex. "Did you send two boys to do a man's job?"

The boys tugged on her, pulling her closer to Lex.

"It's not Josh's and Caleb's opinion that concerns me. They love me, and they trust me, but ... are we finished with the note? I told you why, to exchange myself for the twins."

Josh looked up into Gemma's eyes. "The Fibbies lie and cheat. They was gonna grab you and kill us all."

"Yeah," Caleb said. "They don't give a rip about lyin' and stuff like that."

"Caleb," Lex pulled Caleb's chin around until Caleb faced him. "Where did you get this 'don't give a rip' talk?"

"You say it all the time, Uncalex. But don't ya' think ya' should give a rip about Gemma?"

"Yes. Gemma is just about perfect for me. She has the right degree and some experience. I could use a business partner like her."

"I can find my own job, Lex James. And I don't have enough money to buy into your business."

"What if I offer you a full partnership? Fifty-fifty?"

"Like I said, I—"

"For life, Gemma."

"So I'm going to be indentured for life to The American Motto?"

"Yeah. Just like me."

"What's that supposed to mean?"

"That the boys need a mother and I need a partner."

"How romantic. I give you a career-making story and you reward me with two jobs, a nanny and a reporter. Will I be fired if I don't meet expectations?"

"No. I love you."

"You already told me that. But what do you plan to do about it?"

"Could you ever love a man like me?"

"One like you? Certainly not. Because I already love you, Lex James."

Josh pulled away from his huddle with Caleb. "Uncalex, in the movies this is the part where—it's really gross—but they always kiss."

"Yeah." Caleb said. "And all the people clap and whistle."

Lex closed the distance between them. "We wouldn't want to violate movie protocol and disappoint the boys, would we?"

"I don't know. You tell me."

"You mean tell you like this?" He kissed her.

Or did Gemma kiss him?

* * *

Who kissed whom?

Regardless, Gemma was certain of one thing. Gemma's jinx had ended, buried in the graveyard of dead thoughts that would never again be resurrected. Gemma's jinx had been replaced by Gemma's geniuses, Josh and Caleb ... and, of course, Lex.

He held her shoulders and studied her eyes. "Marry me, Gemma."

"Was that a command or a question?"

"Both."

"You can't do both, Lex."

"Alright then, a question."

"Finally. Four whole days since we met. I thought you'd never ask."

Josh tugged on her arm. "Please say yes. You gotta stay and marry Uncalex. We don't want you to be Aunt Gemma, and we don't want Uncalex no more. You gotta be our mama and Uncalex our dad. If you don't, who knows, we might grow to be like Blade."

"Yeah, Gemma," Caleb said. "We might be crinimals or something if you don't stay and teach us to—"

"Teach you not to tell such whoppers?"

"But we already told whoppers. Do you know how many times we lied to the FBI? That's a crime. We're already crinimals, so we need you, Gemma." Caleb's voice grew soft and low. "We love you, Gemma."

Josh on one side, Caleb on the other. Two sets of arms around her waist. Lex's arms circling her shoulders.

Gemma Saint was trapped, a trap with irresistible bait. She looked down at the boys. "I love you both ..."

She focused on the warmth in Lex's blue eyes, clearly visible in the residual light from the house.

"I love you too, Lex. Yes. I'll marry you. Y'all shoulda' known that."

"Y'all? Do you mean all one of me?"

"No. All three of you."

Chapter 34

Twelve hours later.

Gemma raised her head from the back of the couch in Lex's living room and grimaced as a cramp knotted the muscles in her neck. Her arm muscles tried to spasm too. How long had her arms been draped around the two rascally angels tucked against her sides?

Sometime during the short night, Josh and Caleb had crawled onto the couch and nestled in beside her. Their heads had slumped forward revealing two identical cowlicks on the crowns of those tiny heads stuffed with big brains.

Had those incredible minds gotten them into more trouble yesterday or less? Probably a little of both. Regardless, these two boys had saved Gemma's life and wormed their way further into her heart, all the way to that place where her deepest love and loyalties resided.

They were going to be a handful. Certainly more than a half-grown boy like Lex could handle. But they *had* forced Peter Pan to grow up.

Now, Gemma needed a place to stay until the day when this would become her home. No way would she go back to her duplex in Madras. Not to live.

Maybe she would take KC's offer to stay in her spare bedroom until the wedding. It was a lot closer to Lex's place than Madras.

Resolving that issue, her status in WITSEC, and getting assurance that Lex, the boys and Gemma would be kept safe, were on the agenda for today.

Cody had been benched by his boss and sent back to the hospital to recuperate from his head injuries. But rumor had it that he'd taken some things to work on while in the hospital. So far, there had been no signs of permanent brain damage. Another marshal took Cody's place and Cody had made sure it wasn't Marshal Shaw.

Lex's agenda, on the other hand ...

The Windows message-arriving alert sounded from another room.

Gemma wiggled from between the boys, replaced her body with couch pillows, and covered the boys with the throw blanket.

Josh and Caleb both sighed but didn't wake.

The soft sounds of someone working on a keyboard came from the study.

She tiptoed to the study door.

Lex had already started work on her story. And the fingers on that keyboard were wide awake, typing at a furious rate.

She and Lex had dozed off on the couch around 3:00 a.m., after Gemma finished answering Lex's questions about the conspiracy. Sometime during the night, he had covered her legs with a throw blanket and either went to his bedroom or, more likely, begun work.

Gemma sauntered into the study. Maybe he would give her a status report.

He hadn't spotted her yet, so she slipped behind him and—her foot slid out from under her. Gemma dropped to the hardwood floor with a thump. Probably bruising her rear in the fall.

Lex swiveled in his office chair. "Gemma, are you okay?"

"I think so."

The offending object lay beside her feet. The sheet of printer paper she had stepped on had turned the polished wooden floor into a sheet of ice.

Lex stood and gave her his hands.

Gemma took them and let him pull her to her feet, but Lex continued pulling until both of his arms wrapped around her.

That breath! "Lex, have you been eating anchovies laced with horseradish."

He pulled one hand free and covered his mouth.

He'd obviously worked since three o'clock and neglected all personal hygiene.

"You know something? You need more than a wife around here. You need a mother or Supernanny."

"That's a fine thank you for helping you up."

"It was your slovenly ways that put me down there. And it's obvious you didn't brush your teeth this morning."

"Morning? Yeah. I guess it is." He glanced at the clock on the wall. "8:00 a.m. to be exact."

"What have you been working on?" She tried to give him her coy smile, but how does a person express uncertainty in the face of a chemical warfare attack?

"Been working on the biggest story of my life."

"Do you mean the story about how you got your boys to con a naïve, soft-hearted woman into agreeing to marry you?"

"Not exactly. I mean the story about the saints marching in."

"Please tell me you didn't fill the headlines with puns that use my name."

"Sorry, can't tell you that."

"Lex, my school years were filled with smart alecks making off-color puns about Gemma Saint. Shall I give you a sample?"

"No. I've got my own. Come here and you can read them for yourself. The front-page stories are already published and I'm working on an editorial."

Gemma scanned the home page on The American Motto's web site. "When the Saint Comes Marching in to DC? Subtitle ... you don't want to be in that number when the saint starts naming names."

"D-O-J, D-O-J. There's a fountain of corruption deep and wide?"

"And look at your editorial. Jesus loves the little children, but the FBI doesn't. Seriously, Lex, are you trying to use every song you learned in Sunday School?"

"Not every song. Keep reading."

In a black operation aimed at preventing President Gramm's re-election, a group of undercover FBI agents, under the direction of Max Carr, Deputy Director, made several attempts to kill Gemma Saint and me. To lure me, they kidnapped my twin boys, who are only four years old, and then tried to kill them. While I resent it when people try to kill me, I will do them serious harm if they bother my twin boys. But, as it turned out, the FBI was no match for the twins who disabled an FBI agent and then escaped, bringing me the identification of all the men who kidnapped them. Besides the corruption in the DOJ, there are other reasons to clean house, reasons such as incompetence and
...

"Lex, you're painting certain FBI members as fools. They aren't going to be happy."

"Don't worry. We know who most of the bad apples are. Besides, Cody has already set up U.S. Marshal protection for us."

"So, I go from a phony placement in WITSEC, when I didn't need it, to real witness protection because, not organized crime, but the Justice Department wants to kill me?"

"That pretty well sums it up. I'm trying to put some people in DC in the hot seat, forcing them to take action against the alligators swimming in their swamp. By the way

... do you know what the name Maximillian Carr actually—let me break it down for you. Maximillian is a word meaning great. Carr comes from an old English word borrowed from the Norse. It means swamp."

"Are you saying the actual meaning of the name of the man responsible for this conspiracy is *great swamp*?"

He turned toward his desk, grabbed a box of breath mints, and popped one into his mouth. "Ironic, huh? This conspiracy needs to be portrayed as what it is, such an egregious violation of federal authority that it must be cut out like a cancer. But, with all the entrenched bureaucrats, we may need something systemic, like chemo."

"Or some new treatment, like immunotherapy. Something that targets the cancer. Have you gotten any feedback yet?"

Lex turned from his desk to her again and nodded. "My crew at the office says the phone is ringing off the hook— The Daily Signal, The Heritage Foundation, The New York Post, and the Wall Street Journal. Now, other mainstream media outlets have caved and started calling. They're afraid to ignore this."

"That's because it's too big to ignore. The DOJ, probably with the help of certain Congressmen, Senators and other bureaucrats, planned to control the next presidential election. They could have changed the whole course of the nation. And you laid out the conspiracy, names included. I'm impressed, Mr. James. But, you know, by the end of the day the cable news networks will be calling for interviews."

"Maybe. But they get no interviews unless you're there with me. You're at the center of this, Gemma. Just like you've been at the center of my life, and the twins' lives, since you knocked on our door."

The words she prayed before knocking on that door returned.

There must be a reason why You've allowed all this to

happen to me. Please, God, show me what you want me to do.

The past three days had confirmed the answer. Three people needed her, and she needed them more than Gemma Saint had ever needed anything on planet Earth.

She slid her arms around Lex. "I wish we could just go somewhere quiet, by ourselves, and forget what's going to happen for the next several weeks or months." She pressed an ear to his chest.

His heart was still beating, strong and rather fast. Yesterday, there had been no guarantee it would be beating at all.

"If we could do that, where would you want to be today?"

"Y'all really wanna know?" She slowed her drawl to a crawl.

He smiled. "All one of me? I wouldn't have asked if I hadn't."

She resorted to her coy smile. "I'd want to be with you and the boys in a big Bayliner, throttle wide open, flying across Lake Billy Chinook with the water sizzling under the hull ... and no helicopters in sight."

"I thought you were afraid of water."

"Only of being *under* water. But some frog prince came along and cured me of that. Well, cure might be a stretch. He reduced it from a phobia to a rational fear."

"Frog prince? What happened when you kissed him?"

"He took me on a wild boat ride. Can we do that again, minus the pyrotechnics?"

"Sorry." Lex shook his head. "We can't buy a boat until we pay for those nice people's boat we stole, the one that got blown to bits."

"Lex, I think the Great Swamp should pay for that boat."

"Yeah. He needs to pay for a lot of things."

Chapter 35

Max Carr had heard nothing from Blade Sikes since they had invoked plan B and found KC Daniels involved, helping Saint and James.

Kidnapping was a serious offense. This little exercise in persuasion, by nabbing James's kids, needed to come off without a hitch or there would be serious repercussions.

Any further appearance of failure in Blade's plan and Max would cut the whole black ops team loose and dissolve all ties to himself and other senior-level FBI.

But who could he blame if plan B failed? To be sure, President Gramm had enemies, but blaming them would give all the right-wing conspiracy nutcases enough fodder for a stack of stories and, at the top of the heap, would be the charge of interfering with a presidential election. That charge would hit too close to home, the office of the Director of the FBI or his deputy, Max Carr.

Plan B must succeed, and he needed a progress report from Blade. Though their last call hadn't ended on a positive note, Max needed to reach Blade before activities of the day started. 9:00 a.m. in DC was 6:00 a.m. in Oregon.

He keyed in Sikes's number.

"Hello."

Static crackled through his speaker. Not only was that unusual, it was hard to hear Blade's voice.

"Sikes, have you got thunderstorms in your area?"

"No, I thought maybe you did in DC."

He didn't reply. Something wasn't right. Max couldn't put his finger on it. Maybe things weren't going well with plan B. "What did you do with Ms. Daniels?"

"She's still alive, if that's what you're asking. What do you want done with her?"

"We can't allow her to talk. Get rid of Daniels, Saint, James, and the kids."

"To say Daniels death will be investigated is an understatement. On whose authority am I doing all this killing?"

What was Blade asking and why? It was almost as if he was trying to—maybe Max wasn't talking to Blade.

That thought sent a shiver between his shoulder blades. A muddle of thoughts swirled in his mind. One thought separated from the mixture, self-incrimination. Max had done a thorough job of that in his last few sentences.

"Well?" The man on the other end was waiting.

Max needed to end the call. But if this really was Blade, Max didn't want to do anything rash and upset all their plans when they were so close to completing them.

If he could just ask the right question … "Who are you going to have kill the kids?"

"I'll do it. Can't ask one of the wimps."

That didn't work. What did Blade know that an imposter wouldn't? "How's Kirby doing?"

"Kirby's dead."

"What about Petrelli?"

"Dead too."

"Who's alive out there?"

"I am."

"And who are you?"

"Funny, I was about to ask you the same question."

Max terminated the call. It wasn't Sikes. If the man could be believed, the team members were dead.

From the start of the mission nearly everything had gone wrong. Was the team jinxed? Was there something protecting Gemma Saint? Something that jinxed anyone who targeted her?

Regardless, the primary purpose of the mission had failed. Not just one, but *all* the witnesses were still alive ... according to the man impersonating Blade Sikes.

Blade's failure would cost Max his promotion and his career. If he stayed in DC, he'd be relying on the DOJ's protection to keep him out of prison. He'd had that protection in the past but, since President Gramm's election, DOJ cover-ups were being exposed. Staying might cost Max his freedom.

It was time to invoke Max's personal bail-out plan. But he had never let a person cross him and get away with it. And it galled him to think that the first to do so would be Ms. Saint, a young intern at U.S. News Network, who had been shoved into WITSEC to bind and gag her.

A nobody like Gemma Saint should not be allowed to end the career of the Deputy Directory of the FBI without paying a steep price.

And you will pay, Ms. Saint.

Chapter 36

Three weeks later, Washington, DC

Their mission was simple. March into DC and convince the House Judiciary Committee of the conspiracy against the President. Then get home. Gemma had a wedding to plan.

As their limo rolled down Constitution Avenue toward the Capitol Building, the thought of sitting before a Congressional committee and being grilled sent Gemma's heart galloping. What if she said the wrong thing? What if she really blew it and no one believed her. What if the whole thing turned out like Marsh McDowell's trial?

Gemma placed her sweaty hand in Lex's cool, dry palm. Lex, when he wasn't teasing her, always seemed to be able to calm her.

He glanced down at their clasped hands, where an engagement diamond sparkled on Gemma's ring finger. He smiled.

Lex's shoulder pressed against hers when the limo driver turned left onto 17th Street.

This wasn't the way to the Capitol or the house office buildings. "Sir, where are you taking us?"

The driver's eyes appeared in the rearview mirror, peering into Gemma's eyes. "I thought you knew. President Gramm wants to see both of you before you meet with the Judiciary Committee."

The president? She looked up at Lex.

He shrugged. "It's news to me too. But, it doesn't surprise me."

"I guess he does have a lot at stake here. It's only twelve months until the conventions."

"Yeah." Lex said. "Gives him about ninety days max to tell the world if he's going to run again ... or not."

They turned again and passed through two security gates before the driver stopped near the entrance to a building on their right.

"If I was the president and you were the first lady, I couldn't put you through that jungle they call an election. I'd bail, Gemma."

"I could take it, Lex. It couldn't be any worse than the things Blade and his men said to me."

"Maybe not. But the whole world didn't get to hear those things."

Beyond the entrance, a familiar building profile peeped over the top of the nearest building. Around all the buildings were gardens, grass and trees, a park-like setting.

They were sitting beside the West Wing of the White House.

The driver unbuckled and twisted in his seat to face them. "Just show them your passes and ID. They'll take you to the Oval Office where the president is waiting to see you."

Gemma slid out of the limo and waited for Lex. "I don't know what to say to the President. I wasn't expecting this."

"He asked to see us," Lex said. "He'll tell us why and then you'll know what to say."

A young man in uniform met them at the door.

Then a pleasant receptionist greeted them in a lobby that was smaller than Gemma had imagined. But, filled with smiling faces and light-hearted chatter, the West Wing seemed like a friendly, comfortable place to visit or work.

After checking in with ROTUS, another young man escorted them down a hallway and around a corner to the Oval Office door.

Gemma had seen the president at an event, while she worked for Marsh McDowell, but had never met him. That looming event sent her heart into double time.

When they entered the office, a smiling President Gramm stood and walked around his desk to meet them. He stopped near the presidential seal woven into the carpet and shook their hands.

His warm smile faded. "Gemma, Lex, I feel so terrible about what my Justice Department did to you. From your reports in The American Motto, it appears that if the conspiracy had succeeded, you two wouldn't be here and I would not have sought re-election."

That sounded promising. "Mr. President, does that mean you are going to run again?" Gemma asked.

"It means I'm seriously considering it. But there's more to that than the conspiracy."

Lex nodded. "You mean having to deal with bureaucrats like Max Carr, the great swamp?"

President Gramm chuckled. "Irony of ironies. It's a wonder some political pundit didn't decipher that before now." Again, his smile faded. "The swamp analogy is a good one. Sometimes the swamp is a large alligator bent on eating you alive. At other times, it's a horde of mosquitos, acting in concert, wanting to suck the political life blood out of you. But my concern is more for Mandie than me. There are constant threats. Most are stopped by the agents before reaching her ears or eyes, but not all. Then there are the disgusting rumors spread about her. Rather than defend the truth, most people in the media just fan the flames. And in this Internet-driven climate, everyone seems to be flaming. How could anyone do that to the First Lady of the United States? Mandie is the kindest, gentlest, most gracious woman I've ever known. And, if I do say so myself, for our age she is one hot babe."

The President's smile returned. "Another reason I wanted to meet you two is to thank you. I don't know if our FBI is slipping or if it's you two and your brilliant boys, but—"

Gemma waved her hand with the engagement ring. "They're almost my kids. And they are brilliant. Don't ever try to play chess with them."

"I certainly won't. I get my fill of playing strategy games while sitting behind this desk. But I have a feeling that before all the dust settles on this investigation, you two will be back and I may get a chance to meet those twins. If I do, any advice?"

Gemma laughed. "Don't let them point a squirt gun at you."

"Yes, I read about that. Incredible."

The young man who escorted them in appeared in the doorway. "Mr. President." He motioned to Lex and Gemma.

The president nodded. "It's time for you to head down the street to the committee meeting. I'll be praying for you. Half of the committee will be your friends, as will the chairman. The other half—well, that's why I'll be praying for you."

Forty-five minutes later, Lex and Gemma had been sworn in and sat side-by-side in the conference room. They had been seated in a row of small desks, each equipped with a mic.

Lex and Gemma faced a row of committee members in seats elevated above where the two sat.

The committee chairman, Congressman Willard Wyatt from Georgia, sat at the center.

A curtain drawn across the back covered the wall.

Gemma would not be intimidated by the fact that she had to look up at the committee members above her. They were no better than she was. Maybe she needed to do something to demonstrate her feelings on that subject.

As her sense of empowerment swept over her, she glanced at Lex.

Alarm spread over his face. "Gemma, whatever you're thinking, I'd recommend cranking down the intensity. It scares me when you look like that."

"Like what? I need to know so I can learn to intimidate you."

"Just be careful."

Chairman Wyatt opened the hearing with a rap of his gavel. "We've all read your written statements so let's go straight to the questioning by committee members. We will start with the gentleman from Illinois, Mr. Bane."

Bane's thinning gray hair hung shaggy over his collar, giving him a seedy look. His leering eyes added to Gemma's impression of the elderly man.

She'd seen the same look in Kirby's cloudy eyes.

Congressman Bane glanced at his notes, then studied Gemma's face for a moment. "Ms. Saint, tell the committee why you were placed in WITSEC." His eyes roving over her made a clear statement. He would like to join her in WITSEC, but it wouldn't be protection that he offered.

Gemma shuddered and looked at Lex.

He mouthed the words, "It's okay, Gemma."

"Mr. congressman, the DOJ, more specifically, the FBI, said that my testimony in Marshall McDowell's trial in district court had implicated Joseph Castellano in election fraud and certain other crimes. They convinced me that he would never forget, that he was vindictive, and that he would retaliate. In short, that he would kill me."

"That must have been terribly upsetting for a young person. Thank you, Ms.— "

"Now, congressman, do you want to hear the real reason the DOJ put me in WITSEC?"

The gavel came down. "Ms. Saint, the protocol here is that the committee members ask the questions and you answer, not the inverse. Do you understand?"

"What I understand Mr. Chairman, is that this gray-haired gentleman, and I use that term loosely, has been leering at me since I walked into this room. Then, when I started my testimony, he started treating me like a child. Now, he's trying to prevent me from telling the truth to this committee."

Wyatt's gavel came down with a crack. "We will take a ten-minute recess. And you, Ms. Saint will come with me."

The frown on Chairman Wyatt's face said Gemma had blown it. But had she disqualified herself? She was about to find out.

After she stood, Lex hooked her arm. "Stand your ground, Gemma. But you might want to dial back that temper of yours a few degrees."

He grinned.

Gemma didn't.

Should she punch Lex or kiss him? He could be so exasperating. But Gemma had a bigger issue standing a few steps away with his hands on his hips.

As she approached the Chairman, he pointed to an exit door, then turned and strode through it.

Gemma followed.

The door led to a hallway where a few people walked by, seemingly oblivious to them.

"Gemma, you must keep your emotions under control."

"But that old goat is—"

"We know about that 'old goat'. His behavior is catching up with him and may end his political career. However, that's not on today's agenda. But your behavior, young lady, already caught up with you. You must act respectful toward the committee members and follow our protocol for taking testimony, or I will have you escorted out. If you mind your manners, you will get to tell any part of your story that you feel is necessary. I assure you. When other members of the committee question you, they will elicit the whole story from you and Lex, giving you some freedom in telling it ... or so I've been told. Now, can I expect your cooperation?"

"Yes, sir." She would act respectful, but it would be just that, an act.

When they entered the committee meeting room Gemma was the girl coming back from the principal's office after getting spanked, or whatever principals were allowed to do to kids these days.

Lex had taken his seat, and his eyes roved over the notes he'd placed on his desk.

She focused on him as she walked to her seat, though a hundred pairs of eyes were probably watching her, studying her cheeks, which were probably glowing pink.

One pair of eyes were undoubtedly leering. Half of the other eyes hoped she would stumble and fall on her face. The remainder were what kept her going. They were the people silently rooting for her. The men and women who wanted truth and justice and believed President Gramm was the nation's best hope for getting it.

In a few moments, Chairman Wyatt pounded the gavel and called the meeting to order.

"Mr. Chairman?" The old goat's voice.

"Your time is up Mr. Bane. We now go to the congresswoman from New York, Ms. White."

The rather large woman from New York seemed to have an oversized estimate of herself. And her reputation as an opponent of President Gramm was well publicized. She had focused on Gemma's story about being taken by the FBI undercover team in their black operation.

"How do you expect me to believe your story, Ms. Saint? I'm inclined to disregard your written testimony."

"You've never let truth get in your way before." Gemma paused.

Ms. White drew a sharp breath.

Gemma continued. "Your reputation precedes you. Frankly, I don't expect much out of you, congresswoman."

"Mr. Chairman," the congresswoman glared at Wyatt. "Are you going to let her—"

"Ms. White, think about it. She answered your question with precision. Please confine your questions to the facts, not your personal feelings and, perhaps, you won't get testimony that you don't like."

The sour expression on the congresswoman's face told Gemma to steel herself for what was coming.

"Frankly, Ms. Saint, I find your story not believable. You must have fabricated it. How could you have killed a trained, seasoned FBI professional?"

Gemma blew out a blast of air and frustration. "Congresswoman, I'm not at all happy that I had to do that, but thanks to corruption in the FBI, I took out two FBI team members, one with a squirt gun and a sand wedge, the other with a .38. And, if you still have doubts, I'm quite capable of taking you—"

"Gemma, stop!" Lex jumped to his feet.

The chairman rapped his gavel. "Order! We will have order. Sit down, Mr. James."

The congresswoman's surprised look changed to a condescending smirk. "May I remind you that you are under oath, Ms. Saint."

Gemma glared at the arrogant woman. "Then, may I remind you, that I wasn't lying."

The congresswoman jerked her head back as if Gemma's reply had been a slap to her face.

Lex covered his mouth with a hand.

The muffled sounds of chuckling came from committee members.

"Your time is up, Ms. White. We'll move to the gentleman from Texas."

Gemma hid her smile with her hand and a fake cough. Maybe there was hope for a measure of justice, despite obstructionists like Ms. White.

"Hello, Gemma. I'm Congressman Hall and, like others on this committee, I want to offer my apology for our government allowing such an atrocity to impact your life. And I want to congratulate you for your courage and heroism." He paused.

His personal greeting won Gemma's trust. Hopefully, his questions would not betray it.

"My questions will focus on the reasons you were viciously attacked, who was involved, and what they ultimately wanted to accomplish. I've read the written testimony you submitted, explaining that you were placed in WITSEC to silence you. If you had been silenced, why would members of Department of Justice try to kill you?"

"Congressman Hall, I could prove that the charges against Marshall McDowell were false. We had evidence that the 302s the FBI used as evidence had been edited, after the fact. The FBI needs to join the twenty-first century and record their interviews, if you ask me."

"Ms. Saint," the chairman said. "No one is asking you. Let's stick to the facts and keep your opinions to yourself."

"Yes, Mr. Chairman." She paused. "The illegal campaign contribution charges were contrived by the federal prosecutor based on recorded conversations Marsh had with friends, obtained by, in my opin—uh ... they appear to have been obtained by illegal means. These were recordings of conversations at barbecues and dinners where they chatted about the election. Since Marsh donated to the Gramm campaign, the prosecutor said that when these friends eventually donated, Marsh was guilty of using straw donors. When Marsh told federal agents he didn't use straw donors, the prosecutor added other charges against him, lying to the FBI. Some of these charges used the edited 302s. Marsh didn't lie to the FBI, but they said he did and they compounded everything they could to create still more charges. I testified to Marsh's innocence, but the same prosecutor, using the phony 302s, spun my testimony into evidence against Marsh. During my testimony, I mentioned other donors, among them, a crime boss from New York, a man who had his own selfish reasons for supporting President Gramm."

"So they used fear of retaliation from this mafia-type, Castellano, to force you into witness protection?"

"Yes. I was a bit naïve in my first ever testimony in federal court. But now that I was wise to their games, the prosecutor did not want me on the stand. When Marsh's appeal was heard in the retrial, certain people in the DOJ feared my testimony for two reasons. First, it would likely free Marsh McDowell and second, it could bring indictments against them. They feared it enough to plan to kill me."

"Ms. Saint, most of us know this but, for the record, explain to the committee why members of the DOJ wanted Marsh in prison." The congressman pursed his lips and waited.

"We all know that President Gramm, as a candidate and since his election, doesn't get fair coverage in the media. The big media outlets, including most of the cable TV networks, despise him and his politics. They are vicious in their attacks. Marsh McDowell and his U.S. News Network was the only source of unadulterated news, the only source of objective reporting about this administration. Most experts believe it was U. S. News Network's fair coverage of the campaign that pushed President Gramm over the top and got him elected. Those in the federal bureaucracy that oppose the president will do almost anything to either prevent him from running again or insure that he loses if he does decide to run."

"That's quite an indictment of our government, particularly of our Justice Department. Can you give us the names of the guilty parties, those who were complicit in the attempt on your life?"

"Yes. Some of them. Lex James, my fiancé, heard other names, and my former inspector in WITSEC, Marshall Cody Cottrell, whom they also tried to murder, can give you more names and further corroboration of those involved in this conspiracy."

"Conspiracy? I object!" The woman from New York was on her feet.

Chairman Wyatt rapped the gavel. "For the third time, may I remind you that you cannot object, Ms. White. This is not a court of law. Now sit down, or I'll have you escorted out of here."

"You may continue, Mr. Hall."

The congressman from Texas took a deep breath and exhaled slowly. "Who were the members of the FBI team who allegedly tried to kill you?"

Gemma iterated through the list of names and ended with their leader, Bladen Sikes.

In the seats behind Gemma and Lex, pens rasped on paper and pages of notebooks turned.

"Ms. Saint," Congressman Hall said, "Can you give us the name of the person in the DOJ who ordered this assassination attempt?"

Silence spread throughout the conference room. It became so quiet that when someone coughed it sounded like an explosion.

"Yes, I can. But Lex heard it firsthand."

"We understand that. Please give the committee the name."

"The person authorizing and overseeing the murder attempts on me, Lex James, our twin boys, Josh and Caleb, KC Daniels, and U.S. Marshall Cody Cottrell was ... the Deputy Directory of the FBI, Maximillian Carr."

The room remained silent only for a few more seconds. Then reporters seated behind Gemma bolted for the doors.

Lex's voice rose over the tumult of running feet and slamming doors. "There you have it. *Max Carr*. Which interpreted means *great swamp*. And if you want to question him, you'll probably have to go to South America to find him."

Chapter 37

Two weeks later, Cove Palisades Marina, Lake Billy Chinook

In the warm sun, Gemma sat on a long bench by the marina, one arm around Josh, the other around Caleb.

Lex was deep into negotiations with the man holding a clipboard. If Lex was satisfied, the houseboat floating in front of them would, in one more week, become their honeymoon suite. After Gemma and Lex spent three days and four nights on the boat, they would pick up the boys for the remainder of the week.

The marshals and local police were gone from Lex's place and KC Daniels' house. The need for protection left when Max Carr left the country. With President Gramm reluctant to appoint a special counsel, the House Judiciary Committee was busy smoking out other members of the conspiracy.

These people were far too busy covering their tracks and destroying incriminating evidence to worry about Gemma Saint.

But Gemma had more important matters to dwell on.

Lex looked their way and motioned for them to climb on board the houseboat.

Unsure about what he wanted, Gemma pointed to the boat.

Lex nodded.

Josh and Caleb had already decrypted Lex's signals and each tugged on one of Gemma's arms. "Come on, Gemma. We want to see our houseboat."

"Yeah," Caleb said. "We never been on a houseboat before."

She let the boys pull her to a boarding ramp and they walked single file onto the boat.

Lex called out to them. "It's a fifty-five-foot, ten-sleeper boat. Check it out while I go inside to finish the paperwork."

She turned to yell at Lex before he went inside the office of the marina. "Can the boys swim?"

A sinking sensation deep inside brought feelings of inadequacy and failure. She should have known that. She was going to be their mother.

"Swim? Like two Chinooks," Lex said.

Josh and Caleb dropped her hands and ran into the house part of the boat.

"Boys, find the bedroom you want. But Lex and I get the big bedroom."

Caleb's head stuck out through the doorway. "You gonna sleep with Uncalex?"

What was going through that mind of his. Maybe she didn't want to know.

Josh emerged beside Caleb. "Yeah. You know, Cabe. Like Mama and Dad always did. Cause that's what married people do."

There were no tears now when their mother and father were mentioned. For the boys, the issue was settled. Their mama and dad were happy and waiting for their reunion one day. In the meantime, they had adventures to live and a world to conquer. And the twins waited expectantly for the union that would soon take place, bringing Gemma into their family.

Knowing the boys were happy, and that she was part of the reason, quelled the doubts and fears of failure. She already knew the most important things about Josh and Caleb. She loved them and they loved her.

Gemma walked into the interior of the houseboat. The boys had decided on the room with two bunkbeds near the aft of the boat. Lex and Gemma would have the larger room closer to the bow.

When she stepped out of the cabin near the bow, Lex leaped from the dock onto the boat and slipped both arms around her neck. "So, does this meet with the bride's approval?"

"It's perfect."

"Well, since I told the guy in the office that I already know how to pilot one of these things, he wants to see how I handle it. We're going for a short ride."

"How far?"

"About a quarter mile into the lake. Then we'll circle around, and I'll put it back into the slip."

"You sure you can handle this thing? What happens if you damage it?"

"I pay them with the dowry your father's paying me to take you off his hands."

"So that's why you wanted to marry me. If you married for money, you're in for a big surprise, Lex James."

"Gemma, I'd pay to marry you."

"How much?"

"Well, I'm about to pay thirty-five hundred dollars to rent our honeymoon suite."

"Gee, I was worth more dead than alive ... according to Max Carr's slush fund payment the IG found."

Lex's forehead wrinkled. "That's all behind us now, Gemma. It's as far as the east is from the west."

She forced a smile. "Or as far as the north is from the south. You know, North and South America."

Two heads poked out from the corner of the house. "We goin' for a ride, Uncalex?"

"A short one, Josh."

"A driving test," Gemma said.

Lex took the wheel of the boat and fired up the engine which responded with a deep sound, midway between a purr and a rumble.

Soon, Lex had backed out of the marina and turned toward the middle of the blue-green lake.

"Come on, Gemma. Look at our room." The boys ran ahead of her and disappeared into the cabin near the aft, while the houseboat glided into the lake.

When Gemma rounded the corner, at the rear of the boat, the boys had disappeared. "Come on, guys. I'm not going to play hide and seek today."

At the doorway of the boys' room, a tall figure stood, with Josh tucked under one arm and a gun shoved against his head.

Gemma drew a sharp breath and looked up into the man's face, a face she had seen daily in the news for the past two weeks, Max Carr.

"Ms. Saint, we finally meet. Don't even breathe unless I tell you, or I'll blow his overdeveloped brains all over this deck."

With those words, her terror fled as Gemma reacted to one of her boys being held by a man who had no right to be free, a man who had ordered her murder and, having failed, would do the job himself in a few moments.

She fought her rising, white-hot rage that, unchecked, might drive her and the boys to a sudden death, leaving Carr free to kill Lex.

She couldn't let this story end that way.

"Come here, Gemma. I suddenly have a strong desire to have you near me." His voice came in mocking, sing-song tones.

She didn't move.

"Come, now, or he gets it."

Where was Caleb? Was he okay?

Gemma lifted a foot to take a step closer, but stepped to her left, instead.

Carr turned to face her.

The cabin lay to her left. Behind her was the port side of the boat and behind Carr, the starboard. Both sides were lined with three-foot-high railing.

Gemma scanned everything in her surroundings looking for some advantage.

"Now, Ms. Saint." He pressed the gun into Josh's head.

Josh winced in pain, but he didn't make a sound.

From inside the cabin came a soft voice. "Wonotap oop wye no."

"Sye," Josh said.

"Stop your babbling or ..." Carr's words were as he intended vile and shocking.

The boys probably had no idea what they meant.

"Sye," Caleb said softly.

Gemma's body stiffened.

The boys wouldn't wait for this to play out according to Carr's plan. Something was about to happen.

Josh opened his mouth wide, teeth only inches from Carr's finger.

Gemma took another step toward Carr.

"That's more like it."

The look of satisfaction from a man in total control lit his face with a grin that there was only one way to describe, demonic.

Josh's mouth closed.

Carr yelled and raised his gun to bring the handle down on Josh's head.

Gemma lunged forward.

She drove her shoulder hard into Carr's chest.

Off balance now, Carr's gun struck a glancing blow on the back of Gemma's head.

All three toppled over the railing into the water.

Lightning had flashed in Gemma's vision when the gun struck her. The chilly water removed the stunning impact of the blow.

Gemma scanned the water.

Someone screamed. Not a kid's voice.

The houseboat began a sharp turn.

Josh swam with rapid strokes toward the aft of the boat.

Caleb lowered a rope down for him to grab.

"Help me!" The voice beside Gemma came like the scream of a wildcat. "I can't swim."

If adrenaline hadn't been rushing through her system, sending her heart into a presto rhythm, Gemma might have laughed, because Carr had totally lost it.

Instead of laughing, she swam toward the aft of the boat, where Josh now clung to the rope.

But the aft moved away from her. It moved too quickly for her to catch.

Now, the bow of the boat approached with Lex at the wheel.

Again, Carr screamed for help. Then he screamed obscenities. The pleas and the cursing came in a rapid, alternating sequence as he thrashed in the water.

Lex had kept the boat several yards from Carr. Evidently, Lex was aware of the situation, except for the boys whom he could not see. Worries about them would drive him to panic.

She needed to tell him they were fine.

"Gemma, are you okay?"

"The boys are okay, but Josh is still in the water hanging onto Caleb's rope."

"Are you okay, Gemma?"

"I think so. Just a lump on my head. Help the boys, Lex."

"First, give me your hand."

She did.

He pulled her up to where she could climb the side railing.

She climbed up and onto the deck.

Lex pulled her to the wheel. "Hold it steady. Don't move the wheel or the throttle."

"But Josh—"

I'll get him. Lex sprinted down the side deck to the aft where Caleb stood, hands gripping a rope.

In the water, ten yards away, Max Carr went under. He bobbed up in a few seconds, flailing in the water. "I'm drowning! Help me!" His screeching seemed to have risen another octave.

"Like you helped me," Gemma yelled.

Carr's reply was another plea. "I'm drowning! Can't swim!" His thrashing arms slowed. He went under again.

Lex returned with a boy clasping each of his hands. He took the wheel from her.

Gemma took the boys.

"Mama," Josh reached for her and tears began to flow. Josh seldom cried.

Caleb nodded and leaned against her. "Yeah. Mama."

A love so fierce Gemma could not explain it, contain it, or control it, surged through her mind, her heart ... maybe her soul, wherever the real Gemma Saint lived.

These were *her* boys now, and no one, especially Max Carr, would take them from her.

"Gemma put a hand on Caleb's shoulder. "Caleb, did you see where his gun went?"

"Gun?" Lex said.

"Yeah. After you tackled him," Caleb said, "... it landed on the deck. I hid it by the door so I could get it if I had to shoot him."

"I'll bet he would have," Lex said as he reached out to muss Caleb's shaggy blonde hair.

Gemma stood, a boy's hand in each of hers, and nodded toward the man in the water. "What do we do about him? Do we let him drown?"

Max went down again. Was that the third time? Regardless, he bobbed back up. His arms were slowing. Coughing and choking now, he wouldn't last much longer.

"We were complaining about a corrupt Justice Department," Lex said. "What Max Carr planned was no true justice. Maybe we should give him a taste of the real thing. I'll get his gun. When I give you the signal, Gemma, toss him the life ring." Lex paused. "Here's my cell. Dial 911. I'll keep our buddy, Max, in the water until the police arrive, and I don't care if he gets hypothermia while we wait."

Caleb looked up at Lex. "If he tries to get out of the water, will ya' shoot him, Dad?"

"If I think he might hurt you, Josh or Gemma, you bet I will, Son."

Epilogue

One week later, Gemma's wedding day

Gemma's wedding ceremony at the Crooked River Ranch Chapel had started a 10:00 a.m. By shortly after one o'clock, the reception lunch ended. Gemma had changed into shorts and a tank top, but left the crystal tiara on her head, and Lex had driven her away, headed north toward the Cove Palisades Marina, where they would get their rented houseboat and motor to some unknown location on the lake.

She'd asked where, but Lex wouldn't tell her.

Now she stood beside him on the dock shifting her feet as a fortysomething couple with four kids walked their way.

"You sure this is a good idea, Lex? After all we did steal their boat and leave them marooned."

"I talked to the guy. I think he's okay with meeting us. He doesn't know what we're up to, but he does know who we are, what we did, and that I want to apologize."

"I hope you get your message across before he punches you out."

"What makes you think he could punch me out, oh, bride of little faith?"

"Well, he's not smiling."

The family was only ten yards away and walking out onto the dock.

"He will be. I guarantee it."

"If you say so."

Lex stuck out a hand. "Hello, Mr. Jackson."

Mr. Jackson took his hand and nodded.

"And Mrs. Jackson," Lex said.

"That's the man that stole the Billy Boy," a girl about nine said.

Lex knelt eye-to-eye with the girl. "I'm really sorry about taking your boat. But, you see, those FBI men that came were actually criminals trying to kill us. So it really was an emergency." Lex stood. "We only intended to borrow your boat but, unfortunately, we couldn't bring it back. The FBI blew it up."

"What did they use?" Mr. Jackson said. "One of those Hellfire Missiles?"

"That's pretty close," Lex said. "It was a thermobaric RPG. Makes a big fireball and a big explosion. But, since the government was responsible, President Gramm said the DOJ had to pay for it."

Jackson's eyebrows pinched. "President Gramm? You sure about all of this?"

Gemma stepped beside Lex. "Yes. We saw the president about three weeks ago. He feels badly that all this happened on his watch."

"Hon," Mrs. Jackson said. "Maybe we *can* believe some of that crud they print in the paper." She studied Gemma for a moment. "Ms. Saint is that a bridal tiara your wearing?"

"Yes. As of today, I am Mrs. James. We're just beginning our honeymoon."

"I wouldn't want to punch a guy out while he's on his honeymoon," Mr. Jackson said. "Unless he blew up my boat, or something terrible like that."

"Maybe you should tell him the rest," Gemma said. She looked up at Lex. "Well, either that or, what is it men say ... put up your dukes?"

"Gemma." Lex glanced at her, shook his head, and pulled the keys out of the biggest pocket of his cargo shorts. "Here are the keys to your new boat. A brand new Bayliner.

Same basic features as the, uh, Billy Boy, but a year newer."
He slid some folded papers out of another pocket. "And
here's the title, free and clear."

Gemma met Mrs. Jackson's gaze. "I know this isn't
really compensation for losing six weeks of summertime
boating, but—"

"Oh, I think it will do." Mr. Jackson smiled for the first
time. "The boat was insured. Our insurance company, after
we haggled a bit, paid off what we owed. So getting a boat
free and clear gives us an extra twenty thousand dollars. I
think that's more than enough compensation for losing six
weeks of boat usage."

It was done. Everyone seemed satisfied. Nobody
punched anybody. Even the kids were smiling as Lex and
Gemma walked to the slip where their honeymoon cottage
was moored.

"Jeremy and Jennifer Jackson," Lex said. "They must
love alliteration. All their kids' names start with Js too."

"I rather like alliteration myself. Gemma James. It has
a nice ring to it."

"You could have held on to your last name. Just think,
you could have been Gemma Saint-James."

"I think I'll pass."

"Here's the boat."

"Lex, are you finally going to tell me where we're
spending our wedding night?"

"Lake Billy Chinook."

She jabbed his shoulder. "Be more specific."

"Okay. There's this inlet, our own private cove, just big
enough for one boat to anchor in. We'll be mostly hidden
from anyone passing by on the lake. We can see the sunrise
in the morning from the bedroom window. But being tucked
in against the bluff on the west side of the lake, the night
begins early."

"Early is good. How far is this little inlet? I don't want to wait forever, you know."

"Twenty minutes after we leave the marina, we'll be anchoring in that inlet."

"So it will be around 3:00 p.m.?"

"Yeah. That means—"

"It means that it'll still be around one-hundred degrees. The boat doesn't have air conditioning. We might need a swim to cool us off."

"I thought you didn't like being in water."

"I don't like my head going under but, after what you made me do to get to that cave, I can stay under for a few seconds before I get claustrophobic."

"Good. There's a rock we can dive from by the boat."

"Correction. There's a rock we can jump from. I don't do dives."

"Then maybe it's time to learn."

"Lex ... I think we have enough on the agenda to learn. Changing the subject, what was Caleb asking you about just before we left."

"Uh, that's not really changing the subject, Gemma."

"Oh. I see. What did you tell them?"

"You know how they get when they start the inquisition. They fire questions at you like bullets from those M4s the Fibbies shot at us. Each question feeds logically off the previous question and some part of the answer. They don't stop until—"

"Until you stop them. Please tell me that's what you did."

"Yeah. But one thing was clear. They didn't think we needed three-and-a-half days to get used to being married. I think they just wanted to be here with us."

"I love them so much, Lex. And I'll be glad to show them ... *after* three-and-a-half days of getting used to being married."

"Did you see what Jarrod and Lindy, at the office, gave us for a wedding card?"

"No. I didn't have much time to look at gifts or cards."

"Well, they made up and printed out a special newspaper using all the articles from The American Motto that they thought we'd be interested in—things we missed over the past week."

"This week did get a bit hectic. Statements to the police and the FBI about Max Carr. Then we had to avoid the media, which drove the reporters into a frenzy. Then there was getting ready for our wedding and my parents coming from Texas."

"Make you a deal, sweetheart."

"You already made a deal today, buddy. And it was the best one you've ever made." Gemma walked down the dock doing her best imitation of a fashion model.

Lex caught up with her and curled an arm around her waist. "And I thought I'd married a humble little introvert, someone mild-mannered, subservient ... well, she's like that until she loses her temper."

"You're about to make that happen, Lex. Subservient?"

"Back to the deal. I'll show you how to steer the boat. You take the wheel on the way to the cove, and I'll read you all the news we missed this week. I'll completely catch us up in twenty minutes flat."

"As long as it's good news. Nothing unpleasant, okay?"

"Only the good news. It's a deal."

Lex stepped through the opening in the railing and onto the deck of their houseboat.

He stretched out a hand to help her.

After Gemma stepped onto the deck, Lex scooped her up in his arms and carried her into the cabin, where their suitcases sat beside their bed.

He set her on her feet and kissed her.

But it wasn't a kiss like their first, by the river. And not like the movie-protocol kiss. It was a kiss full of promise for much, much more. "Lex, sweetheart, let's go find that cove."

He slipped a folded newspaper out of the pocket of his small suitcase. "I'll back out of here then the wheel's yours."

The temperature of Lex's kiss had been warm, but the temperature inside the cabin had been suffocating. Probably near one-hundred-ten degrees.

Gemma took the news paper from Lex and fanned herself while he freed the boat from the dock and fired up the engine.

"It will cool as soon as we're moving across the water. The air above the lake is ten to fifteen degrees cooler than the air temperature at the shore, and the breeze we create will make it a pleasant eighty or so."

A few moments later, the boat headed out into the lake.

Gemma moved to Lex's side and let the gentle breeze ripple her hair and cool her neck.

Lex took the newspaper and scanned the first page.

She took the wheel and looked across the broad expanse of blue-green water. The snow-capped tip of Mount Jefferson jutted up from the western horizon. Cliffs several hundred feet high stood to their left and their right.

The incredible setting drove home the reality of Gemma's blessings. They had replaced the lie of Gemma's jinx. And those blessings started with three people she loved more than life, though she prayed she wouldn't have to prove it again any time soon.

In one four-day span of time, God had orchestrated events that turned Gemma's life in an entirely new direction. Then He had confirmed it was the way she should go. The end result, God had met Gemma Saint's deepest needs, restoring much more than she thought she had lost by being forced into WITSEC.

"It's all yours, Gemma." Lex's voice brought her back to the boat and the lake. "Don't run us aground."

"Which is worse, running a boat aground or getting it blown to smithereens like you did."

Lex ignored her comment and started reading. "Marsh McDowell is free and back at the helm of U. S. News Network. The FBI dropped all charges."

Gemma glanced at Lex who had his head buried in the paper. "That's what the president said would happen."

"And Marsh testified early this week about certain members of the DOJ conspiring with a handful of senators to influence a presidential election."

"When that hit the mainstream media, I'll bet there were repercussions," Gemma said.

Lex nodded. "I know some papers that probably lost half their subscriptions. With the nation polarized nearly fifty-fifty between two opposing political ideologies, Marsh thinks the conspiracy might have worked and, get this, he credits you as being instrumental in stopping it. My wife saved our democratic republic. Who'd have thought—" He looked at her in a strange way she'd never seen before.

There was something that went beyond the gaga eyes Lex sometimes displayed when he looked at her. His eyes were honoring her.

Well, that's what it felt like. And it was a look the Melissa's of this world would probably never see from a man.

She smiled at Lex. "Their conspiracy failed and everyone they tried to kill is alive, while only one member of the FBI team survived, Walker, and he's nearly blind."

Lex blew out a sigh. "The DOJ took it on the chin again. They have to pay reparations for all losses to private parties impacted by the conspiracy. For Marsh, this includes his legal fees and his loss of business. For the Jacksons, it included their new boat."

How were they going to clean up the DOJ, especially an organization like the FBI?

"Listen to this, Gemma. Some FBI agents have secretly asked the House Judiciary Committee to subpoena them, so they can testify about deep-state actors without fear of reprisal by their superiors."

That was the answer to the problem. The FBI would have to clean up itself, inside out. "You know, if there aren't enough good agents left, the FBI will be incurably sick."

"But it wasn't the rank and file that were the problem," Lex said. "Well, not for the most part. It was the leadership."

"What about that handful of senators you mentioned?"

"I was just getting to that. The Senate is considering using Article 1 Section 5 to expel two members who knew about the conspiracy and said nothing. Get this, expelling a senator, has happened only fifteen times in the country's history."

"Other than trying to fill openings in the DOJ, what's President Gramm been up to?"

"That's where I was headed. He's running for a second term."

"That's great. We need him to bat cleanup for us."

"Looks like that's what he's doing. He fired the Attorney General and nominated a replacement. A quick approval is expected. And he fired the Director of the FBI, so Gramm has two top Bureau positions to fill. He wants to take his time and not make any mistakes, so he appointed two FBI agents from the ranks to be interim director and deputy director."

"It's hard to remember what it was like two months ago when our nation was oblivious to the treachery in DC."

"Well, the nation is aware, now. One article says there is speculation that several indictments have already been drafted against at least five conspirators and, after the FBI agents testify, the number is expected to double or triple."

"Lex, we're coming to the end of the Crooked River branch of the lake. Do I go west, or around this point and head south?"

"Swing around the point and go south. Our cove is only about five minutes from here."

She turned the wheel slowly to her left and headed into the Deschutes River branch of the lake.

She steered away from the high cliff on her left and moved into the middle of the channel. "It sounds like the government is well on the way to having the wheels of justice trued up. Maybe this unpleasant episode in our nation's history is almost over."

* * *

Lex looked at Gemma standing at the wheel, wind whipping her dark curls against her perfectly sculpted face, and against her neck and her bare shoulders. His wife, and the mother of his boys, was a ferocious mama bear who would sacrifice her life for those she loved, a woman who loved deeply, with the kind of commitment Lex had sought and not found until that day, two months ago, when she knocked on his door.

"Lex, I said I think this unpleasant episode is almost over."

"I heard you. But, Gemma, there's a pleasant episode in our history that's only beginning. And off to your right, about two o'clock ... there's our cove."

"That didn't take long."

"I thought you said you didn't want it to take long. That early was good."

"I did say that. But ... is everything working out the way you want it, Lex?"

"Gemma, it's a little late for having second thoughts. What are you asking?"

"Everything happened so fast."

"Yeah. Just the way the boys wanted it."

"That's what I mean. Lex ... do you think ... I mean it's not possible the twins could have ... manipulated us a bit ... is it?"

"They latched right onto you as soon as they realized I wasn't letting some dangerous lady into our house. But manipulated? I'm afraid you're going to have to get used to that feeling. The boys are experts at getting what they want through devious means."

"But they didn't set us up, did they?"

"Would it really matter?"

"No. I love you, Lex. That's what matters."

Gemma glanced his way with a strange, almost frightened look in her wide eyes. "Sweetheart, would you take the wheel and park us in the cove. There's something I have to do."

"Are you okay, Gemma?"

"I'll tell you in a minute." She walked down the deck toward the aft of the boat.

"Where are you going?"

"I just had this feeling that ... it's probably not possible, but I wouldn't put it past them."

"Wouldn't put *what* past *whom*?"

"I'm just making sure those two boys aren't hiding in their bedroom in back."

"How would they have gotten to the marina? Besides, KC wouldn't have let them go."

"That's the thing, Lex. If they were determined, KC might not have been able to stop them."

The End

Author's Notes

Alright, alright! Caleb and Joshua were not hiding on the houseboat. They stayed with KC. They did have a plan to get to the houseboat, and it might have worked, but they knew their new parents wanted some time alone.

However, when Lex and Gemma pick up the boys, they're going to demand a lot of Gemma's time—a sharp contrast to her time alone with Lex, but also the kind of time that brings deep satisfaction to a mother's heart.

Back to Lake Billy Chinook, that blue-green body of water with three fingers radiating out from the Round Butte Dam—my first introduction to the lake came from an afternoon boat tour given to my wife and me by my brother-in-law's sister, Linda, and her husband, Jerry Fladoos. We explored the entire shoreline by motorboat, zipping at high speed between points of interest.

The tour began in the mouth of Crooked River Canyon, which is lined with four- to eight-hundred-foot-high cliffs. The cliff on the west side also borders the east side of the Deschutes River branch of the lake.

Bridges that cross the lake near the mouths of these two rivers provide access to the west shore of the lake for those coming from the Madras area or travelers driving Highway 97, which is the main north-south highway through Eastern Oregon. The winding road that crosses the two bridges is lined with some serious cliffs that can send a flatlander's heart into a driving percussion solo. My wife, Babe, though she grew up in mountainous Southern Oregon, says about that road, "Never again."

However, the bridges give access to a remote area where many people own cabins, cabins with no power or running water. The land here is semi-arid, but close enough to the Cascades that there are many stands of pine trees.

Unfortunately, this high plateau provides a great spot for cloud-to-ground lightning when the monsoon air sneaks in the back door from the Southwestern U.S. Each year wildfires, mostly set by lightning, destroy several vacation homes.

Back to the lake—near Round Butte Dam, there are some caves at the shoreline. They appear as narrow slits at the water level. As we motored by, our hosts, Jerry and Linda, pointed out the caves. Immediately, a scenario popped into my head. What if a helicopter approached with a crew intent on killing us? How could we get away?

The answer was obvious. Roll over the side and swim under water to a cave. But what if one of the people on the boat has a phobia about being under water? The idea for *No True Justice* came from that question and that scenario.

I managed to surround that scene with the required story elements and to populate it with an interesting cast of characters. Is it all believable? I'll leave that to my readers to decide.

The twins, Joshua and Caleb were a fun addition to the story. After some research, I deduced that it was possible for four-year-old boys with their intelligence to accomplish what they did in the story.

KC Daniels appears in the story and plays an important supporting role. I only mention that she is an American hero, but don't give much explanation. If you want to hear her story, pick up a copy of my award-winning novel, <u>Voice in the Wilderness</u>. I try to keep the Kindle copy on sale most of the time for $0.99. There you'll see how KC and Brock Daniels risk their lives to stop a president who sees tyranny as a quick way to fundamentally change America.

I hope you enjoyed *No True Justice*. If so, please consider leaving a short review on Amazon and Goodreads. Reviews are hard to come by and greatly appreciated by authors. Witness Protection 3 should release in the fall of 2018.

H. L. Wegley

Don't miss H. L.Wegley's award-winning, political-thriller series, with romance, *Against All Enemies*:

Book 1: Voice in the Wilderness

Book 2: Voice of Freedom

Book 3: Chasing Freedom (The Prequel)

Made in the USA
Columbia, SC
02 September 2021

44757005R00152